CW00481929

Edited 10/2012
First print 12/2012

BOOKSTORE DISTRIBUTION

Place orders via our e-mail.

Printed in the United States of America

Acknowledgements

Several individuals have inspired me to write this novel. It took a long time coming, but now it's finally here. To all of my family members and close friends who's had my back from day one throughout my heartaches and pains and my many struggles. My parents are dynamic people, and I thank you for instilling into me as a kid to never use the word "CAIN'T."

To all of the busy people who took quality time out of their lives to read this book — I thank you for your gracious loving support.

To my good friend Aryn McLemore, who I had the pleasure of meeting while in West Virginia. Had you never taken the time to read over the rough draft, and pressured me to polish it up; I thank you.
I also thank you for the perfect concept for my cover. Man it was a blessing in disguise.

I would like shine some light on the strong team at Crystell Publications who helped this project navigate forward. To my editor and friend; Kay, for showing how to keep it business and professional with a pen and paper. And to Kevin at OCJ-Graphics, I could never overlook your talented expertise and top notch skills; you practically created something out of nothing overnight.

Finally, the most love and appreciation goes out to Crystell for being a blessing to us all. GOD gave you the magic! You could dig in deep and come out with a jewel. I thank you for your belief and support in my style of writing. You are the best.

CHAPTER 1

Capo Dona was the Don I worked for. For some strange reason, he frequently called me Vinny. This may sound crazy, but there were times when I'd have to correct him. It wasn't out of disrespect, but I'd often have to remind him that my name was Vonny. Yet, after a short period of time, I came to the conclusion that the guy Vinny had to have been somebody close to him, or a bonafide friend of his.

Every so often, within the year, we were all obligated to meet up at the Big House. Yeah, that's the nickname for Capo Dona's estate. When comments are made about the size of it, he always says that his mansion, the Big House, is just a small mini-mansion to him. However, to me, he lived in what I called "The Castle," which by the way was a very appropriate name for his residence.

The triple story home ingeniously was built on a cliff that hovered over the Pacific Ocean. All of its ivory marble tiles on the first and second floors were always waxed, which made the high polished glossy finish look a little wet. Instead of concrete, the five car garage had a wooden base finish on it. The plumbing was also solid gold to eliminate rust or any type of mildew build up on the pipes. Everything as well as the other fixtures in the sauna, indoor pool, and on the Astro Turf tennis court were all solid gold.

This home was always immaculately clean and neat. The perfectly manicured flowerbeds and front lawn made the Castle often look ancient to me. Most of the upholstery work on the sofa and chairs were done in a fine, soft, Italian leather, which appeared to be imported from overseas. The flawless fabric was also accented with certain artistic features that attributed to the likes of the affluent taste of my bosses wealth.

My boss's home even had a manmade fresh water fountain. There were live fish in it as well. Just from the various detailed features that went into the construction of the home, I could tell that it would most certainly be an architect's dream home. I had to admit, the place was the nicest establishment I'd ever been to in my entire life. As a matter of fact, it was like its very own little private paradise.

However, now that I've matured and have my own personal understanding of lavish living, I've grown to realize that what I admired about his home some time ago was really basic to those involved in the Big Bosses line of work.

Our conglomerate business meetings are always held on the top floor of the Castle, and generally we used the private elevator to get to the third floor, which is where a large spacious conference room was located. The meetings are the same every time: Rolex wrist watches and the traditional Versace business suits.

On one particular morning, Capo Dona was reading the USA TODAY and drinking his morning cup of black coffee, with a hint of sugar. After a long sip from the brim of his cup, he looked over at me.

"Vonny, this is some good coffee here," he smirked, and continued. "You know, I was just thinking. I like my black coffee like this because it reminds me of my taste in women - rich, strong, and black."

"Is that right?" I asked, surfing the Internet as we waited.

"Yep, that's right…" he nodded, very pleased about his comment. "Vonny, the fellas will be here soon. Go grab a dust rag and clean up a little bit," he insisted.

I didn't move... so after about twenty seconds, he started fussing.

"Why you still sitting there – Boy, make yourself useful!"

"Damn," I murmured, not wanting to be the maid at the time.

While walking to the mini-bar, I noticed a female entering the room. Whoever she was, she immediately captured my attention. From the moment we made eye contact, my hormones began to boil and my stomach had butterflies. It wasn't often that I had this kind of feeling, but it did happen from time to time, or at least when a very attractive female was in my presence. As I got lost in her walk, and the thought of us potentially getting physical, her walk, better yet her entire demeanor affected my sexual desires.

Damn, I've found my soul mate, I thought, as we both smiled at one another. The more I observed her, the more I tried to distract my attention with other things. It was almost as if I were trying to pretend like she wasn't even there. I knew she had to be seeing someone, and though I was lusting over her like crazy, at the time, I didn't even realize I was in a danger zone.

"Daddy, while you have your meeting today, can Kristal and I go shopping?" the beautiful young lady asked.

I was shocked to hear her call the chief cornerstone of our delicate organization dad. And though I was surprised, I showed no type of emotion whatsoever. Instead, I continued on with what I was doing, trying hard not to seem nosey.

"What time are you planning on returning?" Capo Dona asked taking control.

"Five-thirty or sixish," she answered, sounding eager to get out of the house.

"Do you need money?"

"Don't bother daddy," she replied. "My new credit card came the other day," she smiled, glancing over in my direction.

I tried not to look back at her, but I couldn't help myself. Once I came back to my senses, I noticed Capo Dona's expression, and he clearly wasn't too fond of her leaving, or me smiling at her. In a real nonchalant manner, he glanced at his Rolex, and then he looked up at her.

"Miranda, we have gone over this before. Honey, you know I want us to spend more time together; especially with you going off to college next year," he said, sounding sentimental. "We never spend any quality time together anymore. Sweetheart, I miss you so much."

"Daddy, I miss you too, but..."

"Shhhh…. No buts. You know we all we got."

After observing Capo Dona and his daughter for a brief moment, Dexter the butler stepped in.

"Masta' Dona, sorry to disturb you Sir, but your guest have arrived. The limousines are driving up now," Dexter confirmed, dressed in his everyday black and grey suit with long tails.

"I'm talking to Miranda right now, so when they arrive, tell them to wait before coming up," the Don ordered. "Oh, and while they wait, have Mary or somebody serve them some coffee and donuts."

Mary was the newest maid at the Castle.

"Also Dexter, I need you to chaperone Miranda and her friend today."

"No problem Master Dona, Sir."

Looking directly at his daughter, Capo Dona gave specific orders.

"And you, young lady - no funny business," he sternly pointed at her. "Make sure you're back here before supper. Do you hear me?" he questioned in a demanding tone.

"Yes Daddy," she said, giving her dad a soft kiss on the forehead.

Capo Dona affectionately winked at his daughter. Then she quickly sashayed out of the room. The summer dress she wore showed off her perfect hourglass frame to the fullest. Therefore, Dexter wasted no time trailing right behind her. And his rapid movement had nothing to do with him greeting the guest. He'd been with the Boss for some time now. From past experiences, Dexter knew Miranda had a youthful innocence about herself, and her spellbinding sex appeal didn't make his job any easier. Besides, with the way Capo Dona loved Miranda, he knew he had better guard her with his life, or else.

Um, she's marriage material without a doubt. A living angel molded straight from the heavens above, I thought, watching her ass as she switched out.

When I was about done with all of the dusting, Capo Dona looked at me with a real grimace look and literally told me to stay away from Miranda.

"She's off limits, Vonny!" he scolded. "I don't want her involved right now. That's if she's still a virgin, and I'm trying my best to keep her pure from the life!" He reproved, stressing the situation a little too much. I knew where my money came from, and I didn't want to press the issue, so I didn't.

"Sure Boss, if you wish," I said, unable to figure out why he felt like I wasn't a good enough companion for his only daughter.

***

The Dons entered the room. Each were dressed in an extravagant custom made suits. A couple of them wore simple turtlenecks under their jackets, but most of them wore your average shirt and tie set up. As they all eagerly sat at a large cherry oak table to negotiate business deals, Mary brought in a hot pot of coffee. Seconds before she reached the table, out of respect, I stood up to block her path. Immediately, I dismissed her and took the pot of mud from her hands. Tenderly, I placed it in front of a crime boss who wore his hair in long dreadlocks.

"Yo' Son, I don't drink mud Kid!" he expressed, speaking with his remorseful New York dialect.

"Sorry about that," I replied, positioning the pot next to my boss, Capo Dona instead.

"Yo' Son, word to ya' mother. You don't be sorry for jack shit. You mean to apologize, but never sorry. You feel me?" he said.

"Word up! I feel you, Son," I nodded in total agreement.

Suddenly, the room filled with laughter. Every person present laughed at me. Capo Dona rose to his feet to make an announcement.

"Excuse me gentlemen! Excuse me, please!" he repeated, insisting on them giving him their undivided attention. "Fellas," he addressed them, and then yanked on my sleeve for me to stand up. "For those of you who didn't know, or have not seen him yet, this here is Vonny West. And from now on, Vonny here will be carrying out all of the eleven families illicit contracts. After each job is completed, he's strictly to be paid fairly for his services in our disposable business," he nodded, looking around the room.

Capo Dona continued... "Before any type of waste is abolished and done away with, it's very important that we continue to elude the feds. We must also liquidate all of our victims assets, to ensure that they are penniless." As he spoke, Capo Dona stared at the Don with dreadlocks. His face showed that he was serious. "Delroy, is that clear?" he questioned in a brusque tone.

Assuming that Don Delroy was trigger happy, I went with the flow of things, kept my mouth shut, and let history take its course. "I would like all of you to personally introduce yourselves to Vonny. That way he doesn't have to be confused about who's who. After that, we are all going to pledge a toast to our new accomplice."

As he spoke to the group, everyone intensely listened to ensure that they carried out his instructions. "Let us all stand, please."

From right to left all of the crime bosses began to walk around the table to greet and welcome me. The first boss I met was, Don Asante. He was a very gleeful gentleman who was by far, older than me. His cheerful smile made me feel comfortable in his presence. As I noticed eight huge diamonds in his pinky ring, the sparkle from the light gave it a nice kick like never before. The next boss I met was, Don Hugo. He also had a pinky ring; however, his contained seven neatly placed diamonds. Don Hugo was a tall, extremely dark skinned individual with a stocky build. As the next crime boss, Don Malik introduced himself, I noticed how his contrast was clear and sharp. He was classy with a stylistic look about himself. He wore a six diamond pinky ring. Immediately, I noticed he was wearing the latest summer sandals by Versace, which matched his suit. With no time to get caught up in his G.Q. Appeal, Don Devo was next to introduce himself to me. Instead of a hand shake, he gave me a hug, and then said, "Welcome to the family loved one."

His pinky ring was shaped as a five point star, with tiny diamonds in it. The fourth ring gleamed with a twinkle off of a boss named Tang. Don Tang was the jazzy Valentino type that every crime boss gave their utmost respect to. The brown fox coat he wore exercised his ostentatious lifestyle and appeared to cost well over $10,000 at least.

When Don Tang approached, Capo Dona grabbed his hand to shake it, showing his loyalty and respect for the man.

"Nice to see you again, Capo Dona," he said, displaying a mutual honor towards my boss.

I noticed that everyone here today shared a special bond. They respected and loved each other like close brothers would. Very close brothers, which made the ambiance radiant.

Following Don Tang came the middle aged Don with dreadlocks. As he walked, he used an ivory marble cane. He was the boss they called, Don Delroy. We had already familiarized ourselves with each other earlier that evening, so I immediately knew who he was. He wore a moccasin style dress shoe, and because I was a stylish shoe kind of guy, I asked him who the designer was.

"Vonny, this is a John L. He personally made them for my bad feet," he answered with his heavy, East Coast, New Yorker accent. "Kid, I know him personally."

Noticing the three diamonds in his ring, made it obvious that the next person I would be privy to meeting would be the two stone boss. After he introduced himself to me, I happened to glance at his finger, and just as I thought, my assumptions were on point. Don Eastwood told me that they called him Eastwood as a result of the way he handled his .44 Desert Eagle. Then he opened his suit jacket to expose its chrome pearl white handle to me.

"Those are some real nice threads you're wearing," Don Eastwood acknowledged, as he walked back to his seat. Still focused on him, I glanced at his feet, only to discover that we both wore the same type of shoe.

Either I got Boss like qualities, or it's really amazing to see that I'm wearing the same style shoe as a Don, I thought, looking myself over in my dark blue Felani suit. Since he wore his with Versace, his look was costly, but yet and still quite elegant. Don Dante John was the last of the crime bosses I met. He was wearing one single solid Marquise stone in his pinky ring. And real talk, I couldn't help but stare at it as it appeared to weigh in at about two to three karats.

His contour profile was very serious, and he didn't seem like the talkative type at all. In fact, he totally ignored me. Don Dante John shook Capo Dona's hand, and then showing no emotion whatsoever, he went back to his seat next to Don Eastwood.

This gathering was designed for the elite, and the men in this room were considered the Top Dog's, the Godfather's, and the King's of the dirty scandalous urban underworld. Observing them and their demeanor one final time gave me a giddy feeling in my gut. Yet, though they were deemed as the untouchable and ruthless; I still must admit that being in the same room with men who had so much power was chilling to me. But at the same time, exciting. Together, they were the examples of the individuals the government labeled as those who thought they were, "ABOVE THE LAW." With that said, now that it was my turn to join the group, my ego was inflated.

With drinks in our hands, we all stood at the request of Capo Dona.

"To Vonny... our new brother!" He proposed a toast, exercising his strength of leadership among us. All in unison we pledged the loyal code of silence among each other, and then they ceremoniously added me to the family tree.

Wish I could give you more details about the ceremony; however, this is the part I'm not allowed to disclose to the public. This induction was very sacrilegious and historical to me, and thankfully, I have now been baptized into what is called the, *Black Illuminati*, and I'm proud to death about it.

CHAPTER 2

After our meeting, Capo Dona with my help made sure that every crime boss was transported to a private airport and safely boarded the family's Lear jet. After ensuring that each was accounted for, we sent them all on their merry way back to their very own private destinations throughout various parts of the country. Luckily, the process went as smooth as it did.

Once back at the Castle, Capo Dona felt as if it was time to have a very complex discussion about life. What I needed was an understanding of why each Don wore rings with a certain number of diamonds. During our meeting, I was very curious about that, but reluctant to ask questions while the bosses were present; but that didn't change the fact that I still wanted to know what the number of stones worn by each Don truly meant.

Capo Dona sat at one end of the long table and I was at the other. We both felt exhausted from the long day and all the festivities. As my boss sipped on a relaxing drink of white wine, I sat in my lounge chair and remained quiet as he spoke. For some reason, I took a fast glance at the clock on the wall, coincidentally Capo Dona just so happened to notice my glance.

"You know, it's after eight o' clock and Miranda still hasn't made it home yet," he paused for a brief moment, almost appearing to be in deep thought, then he spoke again. "Vonny, whatever you do never try to understand a female," he annoyingly, shook his head.

"Dexter knows to bring her home, right Boss?" I asked, trying to ease the problem a little.

"I wanted her back before supper!" he fussed, pounding his fist on the table. "I never get to really spend any quality time with my baby girl anymore," he expressed, casually twirling around the last corner of wine that remained in the glass. "Vonny, I got fifty states on lock and my own damn daughter doesn't even respect what I say."

"Boss, I'll have a talk with her about that."

"Nawh!" He waved off the thought.

"Capo Dona, what's wrong with you?" I questioned.

"What if they've been kidnapped?"

"Boss, stop playing," I insisted. "I'm sure Miranda's limo will be pulling up any minute now," I responded, thinking to myself that rich folks always had issues. "Capo Dona , if you don't mind, let's get back to why all the bosses rings varied in regards to their stones."

"Okay, you're right. Vonny, let me give you a small idea of who the men are that you're so fortunate to have backing you," he smiled, filling his glass with more of the white wine. "Umm, before I start, would you care for a drink?"

"No sir." I lied, basically trying to prevent the both of us from being tipsy. Surely with all that could go on in our world, one of us had to keep a clear head around here.

After taking in more of the warm liquid with one gulp, he continued.

"Our conglomeration is the most prestigiously honored black organization in this country. You know why?" he asked. Before I could answer he did. "….because we don't snitch or rat on each other. The Family has solidification, son. We are also the best paid underground assassins since the Muslims. We are the best that there is today, when considering the modern gangland murderer. We are also the best that America will ever see or get, when coming from the black perspective. Vonny, that's how we breed each other. Thorough. And that's how I'm going to breed you."

"Is that so?" I sarcastically asked. Capo Dona paid me no mind, it was almost as if he wasn't even listening to me. And without acknowledging me, he continued...

"Don Asante is from the eighth circuit. Don Hugo is from the seventh circuit. Don Malik is from the sixth circuit. Don Devo is from the fifth circuit. Don Tang is from the fourth circuit. Don Delroy is from the third circuit. Don Eastwood is from the second circuit, and last but not least, Don Dante John is from the first circuit.

We have two more colleagues who are ranked higher-up in this familial. You haven't met them yet, but don't worry; they know of you - you just don't know of them yet. However, in due time you will learn to trust me. Now understand that they are very high powered individuals who believe in staying low key and away from problems.

They fall back not because of the problems, but because of the millions of dollars being secretly invested by us all across the globe." When I heard the word millions, my eyes opened real wide. I was like a junky on crack.

"Vonny, I've personally been assigned as your sponsor. I will guide you through the basic detail. At times things may get a little out of hand though," he explained.

"Hold up!" I interrupted, wishing he'd stop beating around the bush. "Just tell me what's going on," I said, feeling agitated.

"They have a lot of dry snitch's, tattletale's, and other people in the different milieu organizations who would love to secretly inform the local, state or federal officials about our activities." His voice began to slur a little, which gave off the impression that he was becoming a little drunk from his second glass of wine. "Vonny, they can't wait to tell on us," Capo Dona had to be feeling the wine, because he totally devoured another glass, never considering his buzz, or reacting to the fact that he'd spilled a little on the table.

"Boss, hold up. Let me help you out here?" I insisted, looking around for a rag.

"Good lookin' out," he said, watching me clean up his mess.

As I continued to wipe up the mess with a small rag, I thought about how Capo Dona was like the father I never had. He was also the only person, while I was in federal prison, to keep money on my books. I admired him because he did what he wanted to do, and there was nothing anyone could say about it. So since I had love for him and our situation, I felt that it was up to me to make sure that he didn't over do it.

"Vonny, where are you taking that bottle!" he shouted.

"To the bar," I said, walking over to the mini-bar totally unconcerned about what he had to say about it.

"Look here you little squirt, I'm grown!" he shouted, intoxicated.

"I just f..."

"I know what you felt," he cut me off, screaming.

"Don't fuckin' yell at me either!" I snapped back at him.

14

Capo Dona tapped on his coat pocket and reached inside of it, which made me real nervous. I didn't know if he was drawing iron or what. So since I'd never raised my voice at my boss like that before, I didn't know how he was taking it. While still digging in his coat pocket, he began to softly mumble under his breath.

"Boy, this is my fuckin' house. You better watch what you say. Shit! Who do you think you're talking to like that...?" he frowned, retrieving a manila envelope from his pocket. He gave me a quick cold stare, then tossed it on the table, as if it were a deck of playing cards. From the bulkiness of it, it looked as if there was some money inside. I figured it was, but I refrained from showing any type of aggression and kept my cool. To act as if having a lump sum of cash like that was the norm for me.

"Go on and take it," he demanded in a nonchalant manner. "It's yours."

Right when I stuffed the envelope in the crotch of my pants, Miranda just so happened to flounce her fast tail in the room. She looked fine as ever and had her hair freshly braided in tiny micro-corn rows.

"Daddy, I'm so sorry for being late," she chimed in. "I had my hair done today and it took longer than usual."

Miranda was trying to explain herself, but it wasn't working. The girl knew that she was in big trouble, so she tried to butter her dad up with a kiss on his cheek. *Can't she see that he is drunk*, I thought to myself.

"I was worried about you. Doesn't your limousine or even you for that matter have a cell phone?" Capo Dona asked, expecting a reasonable answer from her. "Why didn't you at least call home and let somebody know where you were?" he questioned, trying to get the girl to understand her responsibility.

"I said I'm sorry - besides, I was busy," she boldly had the nerve to say. *She done messed up now...* I smirked, looking at Capo Dona . *Yep, I can see a real verbal lashing coming,* I thought.

Capo Dona was so mad that he had to calm himself down. He rubbed both of his temples, while Miranda's little fancy ass thought all that was taking place was nothing more than a joke. She didn't know how serious things were around the house lately, which wasn't entirely her fault, considering the sheltered life she lived. The boss very slowly eased his way towards his young beautiful daughter, and with his eyes that screamed from her lack of respect, he raised the back of his hand and smacked the shit out of her face. Immediately, she had a reality check.

"Young Lady, you think my orders are a game around here!" he yelled, slamming his fist on the table. "Now get the hell out of my face. You disgust me!" She ran directly into my arms. "You will learn to stop playing around with the rules of this house! Do you hear me?"

"Yes daddy," she cried, horrified at her father's sudden rage. "Vonny, let her go!" he yelled.

She ran out of the room. As she held the side of her face, she left the door wide open. I never saw Capo Dona so angry, and since the following day was Sunday, I headed for the door, too. It had been a very long, and extremely exhausting day for all of us, me especially. As I was walking out the door, I paused to give my boss a hug.

"Vonny, the Don's run all of the U.S. Federal Circuits in North America," he stated, giving me something to think about.

When I walked outside, much to my surprise, right by my bike was Miranda. She was standing next to the motorcycle still crying and holding her face. I knew she was not in the mood for a lecture, but I still had to give her words of wisdom.

"He did it out of love, Miranda," I said, straddling my bike.
"What kind of motorcycle is this?" she asked.
"A Ducati 900."
"Could you give me a ride on it one of these days?"
"I don't know, maybe," I told her, starting it up. "Well you take it easy, and be more mindful of your father's words," I advised her before riding off into the night.

Before ever exiting Capo Dona's property curiosity was killing me. I had to know what was inside of the package. While riding down the Castles' long cobblestone driveway, I considered how the day had been a good day so far. Now while riding home, all I had to do was elude the police, because the thought of being pulled over and my package being confiscated or seized by the authorities was a tragic thought.

Rechanneling my thoughts, I finally cleared the residential area and leisurely cruised onto the 91 Freeway marked Westbound, then pushed the engine to a speed well over100 MPH. Always up for a thrill, I made it to Compton in less than ten minutes flat.

***

My G-Momma still stayed in Compton. I can remember ever since my childhood, she always teased me about buying me a sports car to drive her around in, once I got older. That was our thing. G-Momma made a good living for herself by managing an afterhours gambling shack, and a late night whore house, which was stationed in the guest house, located in the backyard of her home. It may sound crazy, but I've seen it all growing up; and all my life I've been around fast money as a result of living in the ghetto streets of Compton. Yeah, those were the good ole' days.

As I rode against the cold chilly wind, which hit up against my nylon ski mask that I wore up under my helmet, I considered the odds. At first, I ignored my first mind that kept telling me not to go over my G-Momma's house, but my gut stayed on me, so I stopped and turned the bike around to head home.

Currently, I stay in Cerritos all by myself, which was much nicer than Compton. As I sat at the stop light, revving up the engine, I realized that the streets were clear all the way down the block, so I punched it after the light turned green, and made it home in just a couple of minutes.

My home was a brand new gated complex with a large oasis of water that served as a pond to a family of ducks. It sits conveniently in the middle of our high priced condominiums. Most were owned by affluent individuals like ex-cops, doctors, lawyers, and nosey old folks. There was a female dope dealer who lived in our private community as well, which is also where I buy most of my "Chronic" from. She drives one of those fancy cars that bounces up and down on those shiny gold rims and 13" inch tires.

As I rode up to the complex, our security guard greeted me, and then opened the gate. Upon entering the property, I rode to my zone, parked my bike in stall #9, right next to my Acura Legend. I walked in my home, marched up the stairs, ran me some bath water, and then checked the answering machine for messages. The first one I couldn't understand, so I deleted it. There were two more, so I listened to them.

"Yo! What's up, Cuzz? Check this out - Eddie is dead. Homey, as soon as you get this message, call me back," the person said as the line went dead.

Lefty was like a brother to me. We went from kindergarten to the twelfth grade together. Eddie and I called our best friend "Lefty Bull," because back when we were youngsters in the old neighborhood, he was the only kid who wrote with his left hand among us all. The Bull title came a few years later. It was when we were much older and he became a very unique knockout artist. Lefty knocked out anybody in the hood who messed with us, so we named him Lefty Bull and the name just stuck with him, even while at Compton High, teachers called the homey Lefty, too.

"Mr. West, please call us back as soon as possible here at our Lakewood Century 21 Office," the next message chimed in.

"I know already, my rent's due!"

Since the water was still running in the tub, I slipped off my shoes and walked back upstairs extremely excited about what was inside the package from Capo Dona. When I unwrapped the envelope, it contained ten crispy clean brand new $1,000 bills. Being that I've never held a $1,000 C'note before actually made me feel like something was wrong. The moment felt odd to me, and ever since I was a child, I'd always dreamed about being paid and full, but never on a level like this.

While holding all ten C'notes in my hand, I felt proud. I sat on the side of the tub, turned off the water, and took off my clothes. I quickly hopped my butt in the bathtub to soak, hoping that no one distracted me while taking a steamy bath. *With this ten grand, my life has just gotten better*, I thought, before dousing my head under the water.

CHAPTER 3

On September the 8th of last year, they finally released me from Lompoc Federal Penitentiary. As I drove to my destination, all I could think about was the fact that yesterday marked the one year anniversary of my release from the federal penitentiary. I must admit that I am real happy about gaining back my freedom. While in the Feds, I knocked out a five year bit for some drugs the DEA planted on me for not turning snitch.

They hit the hood hard, trying to crack down on the illegal usage and trading of firearms and drugs, just so happen, my name mysteriously popped up on a federal indictment. At the time, I had nothing to lose, so I took the case to trial - and lost. An all white local jury did me in. They were all good friends to the prosecuting attorney, which is how I became a walking cadaver that belonged to the federal government.

Now look at me, it's been a whole year since my release from the belly of the beast, and the rules of engagement have changed since then. I almost can't believe that I've been adopted into an elite black syndicate group. Nobody would've ever thought I'd be driving up an old cobble-stone road to a beautiful, huge, grandeur mansion with ten grand in my home safe. I didn't even have a clue as to what all would be expected of me yet; but my goals in life right now is to stay loyal and true to this entourage of underground black crime bosses.

After meeting the Don's, life seems different to me now. I mean, here I am with no knowledge of basically what type of activity needed to be pursued. I have not one skill, but I'm gifted when it cames to street knowledge. My behavior had been rambunctious at times, and I had a quick wit for hustling, which was the only way I survived growing up in the ghetto school of hard knocks.

"Capo Dona," I muffled, speaking into the intercom on the wall next to the front door. While waiting patiently for somebody to let me into the house, I suddenly noticed fish swimming around under the porch. The huge gold fish were all looking up at me like I was gonna' feed them or something. Instead of feeding them, I flicked a dime in the water and made a wish for good luck.

"The door was open," a voice said, giggling at my naïve behavior. Her beauty made me nervous, which is why my hands started to sweat. We both stood in front of the doorway staring at one another for a few seconds.

"Are you going to let me in?" I asked.

The snazzy little well portioned Ebony queen was wearing a scanty one piece swim suit, which immediately got my attention.

"Oh. Sorry. Come in, please. – Come in," she repeated.

"Do you have a name?" I smiled, delighted to be in her presence.

She'd noticed me eyeing her body. And body she had. The girl was fine. Her slim waist fed into the curviest curves I've ever seen. There was nothing about what she was working with that was in disagreement whatsoever, and because I was so captivated in lust, I almost missed it when she told me her name.

"Umm – Excuse me, what did you say?"

"Pam... I said my name is Pam. And you must be Vonny West?" she asked more as a statement. "Miranda and I have been talking about you coming over all morning."

"Well I hope it was all good stuff," I replied real suave.

"Follow me," she said, forcing me into a lustful trance.

Pam sashayed with a confident strut and was quite aware of her perfect figure. I felt comfortable about being escorted by a woman with so much faith in herself, so as I trailed closely behind, I couldn't help but also admire her pretty tanned bow legs, and those voluptuous thick country thighs that were strutting through the house. I followed the auburn colored Ebony queen through the living room, through the kitchen, through the maid's living quarters, and finally we arrived by the indoor pool area. Instantly, Pam plunged head first into the pool with a perfect dive.

"Vonny, over here!" Capo Dona's masseur shouted. I glanced to my right, noticing Miranda waving as she relaxed in the Jacuzzi.

"Miranda," I spoke, nodding to seem mature and professional.

Capo Dona was stretched out on his stomach, talking on his cell phone, and enjoying a morning massage. Since I wasn't dressed for the occasion, I felt a little strange and over dressed. I had on a dark blue cashmere wool suit, with black Romeo hard sole dress slippers, and a matching blue Stetson Derby. My cologne was Burberry.

"Okay that's enough. Thank you," Capo Dona waved his hand to his masseur, then rose up, wrapping his cloth towel around his pudgy waste. "Follow me," he instructed with a serious pitch.

My boss led me to a small lodge that sat deep in the back of his yard. From my many visits, I'd learned that the lodge we were going to was originally a small storage room, but Capo Dona throughout the years had it renovated into a small office cabin. He replaced the old wood with a new cherry oak that constantly gave off an everlasting sweet outdoor aroma. Very softly Sade's song, *Smooth Operatoooor*, serenaded us as we stepped in.

"So how did you feel about yesterday?" Capo Dona questioned.
"Actually, I was overwhelmed," I answered him, when suddenly I noticed a cigar in a solid gold ash tray on the desk.
"Vonny, don't feel for one second like this job is an easy cake walk. If you didn't notice yesterday, let me express that all of the bosses are very serious minded gentlemen. Son, they were feeling you out. So don't let us down, me especially."

He threw a 6x9 black/white photo printout in my lap. The picture of Mobie "Dique" Lewis startled me and gave me the jitters. Not because I was scared or afraid of the thug, because I don't fear no man that can walk and talk like I can; but it's the fact that he was one of the most feared and respected Crips at The Poc when I did my time behind the walls.

"That's a photo of a gentleman named Mobie Lewis," Capo Dona strategically mentioned. "Do you know of him?" he asked me.
"Yep, sure do." I answered, crossing one leg over the other to look more sophisticated. "While I was in the joint, he was appointed as the chief – so he served as the shot caller for all Crip families from

different parts of the country," I explained, giving limited details on what went on in prison behind the walls.

"Well some of our sources just informed me that he's out of prison now, talking and walking around as if he's in the clear."

"Meaning?" I questioned, to get a better understanding. "Boss, this guy, Diques has so much influence and power among the Crips that we may never be able to get close to him."

"Not we... You!" he insinuated.

"He's well protected, Boss," I said, feeling nervous all of a sudden.

"Vonny, every person in this world slips from time to time. You should know that already from past experiences. Besides, he's a snitch!" Capo Dona roared, paralyzing our conversation. "I don't care who he knows or who he's with at the time, he's a rat, so that means that he's gotta go nighty-night. He's a body, Vonny, so get over it. The conglomerate specializes in these types of eliminations. That's why we're the best." He bragged with an arrogant type of confidence.

"If the man's hot, then I don't understand why not let his own people handle him?" I asked.

"They've tried, but failed. On numerous occasions they've had quite a bit of gunplay, but have been unsuccessful every time they've tried to get him," Capo Dona laughed. "Let's stop the games and finally finish him off before somebody else gets hurt. You have ten grand for the mission. After the job is complete, I've been instructed to turn over a blank corporate check to you for you to sign over to yourself in whatever amount you desire for the job. We all know that your role in this isn't the most knowledgeable one, so take it easy and think. The family has your back one hundred percent. We only ask that you use your own ingenuity and expertise when moving about. Don't make us look weak, Vonny," he sharply uttered.

"Is there a time frame for me to complete this project?"

"Yeah. After we get authorization, we want the job done soon as possible." Capo Dona, lit his cigar. " But if you ask me, the sooner the better."

Theoretically, knocking people off is the most hated crime one could ever commit, but in my eye sight to whack a punk ass snitch, common child molester, or a pederast is very logical to me, I thought, watching Capo Dona get up to retrieve a wooden rectangular box from his desk drawer. Once he secured it in his hand, he walked back over towards me.

"Here, open this," he handed me the box, smiling.

Inside the box was a black pistol with a beautiful chrome silencer, lying next to it. The plush red velvet that layered the box, made both the deadly items look harmless and purely innocent.

"That there was my very first piece," my boss smiled with much pride."Kid, do you know I was only twenty-one years old when the man known as your father gave me that piece of iron," he explained. Then added, "I had the heart of a lion back then."

Suddenly blasting out from my impulse, I responded to his comment.

"My father!"

"Yeah .. You see your dad Vinny West was the head of this Syndicate back in the late 60's and early 70's. Of course, you were just about to be born back then."

"My father?" I repeated, not understanding why no one had ever mentioned that to me. "So you mean to tell me that my Pop's was a crime boss?" I questioned.

This was such a shock to me because ever since I was a young boy, growing up in the hood, I never saw or knew anything about my dad. My mom had raised me all by herself in a single parent home. Now don't get me wrong, she did the best she could. God bless her heart. Unfortunately, in the hood at night, things could become rough, so rough, it was almost like being in World War III. There were constant rapid gun shots going off in the streets from gangs retaliating on each other all night long. Then one unexpected evening, my mother laid down for a nap after work. Sadly, she never woke up from her dreams or that nap ever again. And what was more painful to me than anything is that she passed away, holding on to one of the greatest secrets of my life.

I almost could not believe what I was hearing... My father. And after all that I've been through so far in my life, one of the worst things a child could have ever gone through was having to bury his mother at the age of sixteen. To this day I'm still trying to put back the missing pieces of this strange puzzle.

"Vonny, I don't know what to say."

"Tell me Capo Dona, are the Dons' all aware of the mishap from my childhood years?" I asked, curious for all the right answers.

"Sure. But right now isn't the time to allow yourself to get in a sympathetic state of mind. You're a grown man now, Vonny. At this time, we have a very important job to do. There's an imposter on our hands and he's an illegitimate one. The payoff is sweet, so don't fuck it up! After you dust off our victim, be extremely careful. Keep in mind that he's a government witness, and Vonny the feds have multiple informers and spies everywhere, so many that it literally gives me the creeps. Also, don't for any reason try to contact me here until I give you the green light to push forward. The phones may be tapped. Again, don't have any links to this house nor the organization until further notice; and don't for any reason worry about nothing. I'll contact you when it's the right time. And while you're out there, remember to always stay above the law and stay incognito after the hit," he instructed me.

As Capo Dona gave me my orders, he had a profound and very serious look on his face. At the time I was very confused, and had several thoughts scrambling in my head. My reality, or what seemed like my reality of all this was mystified. I mean, here I am the prince of this entourage. In all actuality I was more than eager to delete any victim for reasons that were way out of my control. My boss looked over at me, and I noticed that he started sweating on his forehead a little.

"What are you doing?" he asked, watching me screw on the guns silencer. I think Capo Dona was a little spooked cause he knew that if I was to pull the trigger, nobody would hear the gun go off. A silencer will muffle any gunshot sounds from any gun, without fail.

"You have a guilty conscious about something?" I asked, holding the power, and feeling sort of proud of my bosses sudden acts of nervousness. "Relax..." I told him. "I'm not going to shoot you. I love you too much for that."

He suddenly sipped on an ice cold glass of water, and anxiously swallowed in one gulp.

"I'm not driving around with this thing in a case," I explained. "Business just wouldn't get handled that way, now would it?"

"I agree. I agree." My boss said, taking a strong pull on his smelly cigar again. The odor was turning my stomach over into crank convulsions. "Vonny, have you ever used a heat?" he asked, huddling over me as if he was going to snatch the pistol from my hands.

I pulled back.

"That gun is nothing without self control son. Right now you have the power of people's lives, so use it wisely. Do you understand?" he spoke to manipulate my arrogant behavior. "Vonny, remember to calculate every action before you select the appropriate time to make your move. Before the initial strike, you have to outmaneuver your victim, circulate a little and mingle around a bit. The take down is high-priced so make it look professional. Also, remember; never go into an establishment or building unprepared. You have to know how to exit out fast. A lot of good men end up dead that way."

That's the reason I always give Capo Dona the utmost respect; because he takes time out with me to explain each situation and every detail. Ever since my release from the feds, Capo Dona has taken me in and put me up under his wing. He always gives me positive advice, with good direction, and a well planned out blueprint on how to make it in a today's modern society. With a bogus felony conviction in my criminal files, I have no alternative but to take heed to his advice and use his knowledge as a giant stepping stone towards success.

Capo Dona's cigar was just about to burn out. From my past dealings with important businessmen, I've come to learn that my boss is a true conversationalist. Oh, and the longer the cigar, the longer his conversation's going to be. Now being that the cherry on the cigar was just about to burn out, my time was coming to a close. As I raised my wrist to catch a glimpse of the time, Pam stepped into our meeting, looking like she belonged in a Sports Illustrated with her deeply tanned, dark-reddish brown complexion. Miranda wasn't too far behind and entered shortly after her friend. She was holding a bowl in her hands with some of the finest choice fruits available.

"Daddy always says that some fruit after a good swim keeps the body in shape," she'd smiled, offering for me to help myself. "Would you care for some fruit, Vonny?" she asked, moving the bowl in front of my face. With the way the bowl was positioned, I couldn't focus on the fruit, because all I noticed was her cleavage, resting on top of the dish. "Go ahead, pick one," she insisted. I took a dark plum out and bit it. As I looked down, I noticed that both of the girl's feet were bare, and not fully dry, so they'd left puddles of small, girly footprints on the wooden floor.

Miranda and Pam both had on robes similar to Capo Dona but, Miranda's was white and Pam's was pink. But most importantly, theirs showed every enticing curve on their small framed bodies.

When the girls intruded in on our meeting, the pistol had already been put in my left coat pocket and was concealed.

"Well is that about it?" I asked, reframing from calling Capo Dona boss in front of the young ladies. I stood up. While on my feet, I felt like a professional hit man, even though I was still a virgin to the business, the small artillery brought out a confidence I never knew existed inside of me.

"Vonny, do you have a cell phone?" my boss asked.

"Nawh," I casually said. " –but I have a phone at home."

"Well go home and wait for the word then."

"Sir, I still have to wait for my probation officer to call. You know I'm still on parole..."

Looking over at the girls, who had become inquisitive, he just kind of waved me off.

"Will do then, I'll contact you there," he nodded, dismissing me.

As I made an attempt to leave, the girls didn't allow me to. They insisted that I stay and at least watch a movie with them on the new, 62" wide screen Capo Dona had recently bought. I figured it was the least I could do for being rude. I sat for a short time, but when I thought about my bosses feelings regarding me, and then his daughter, I snuck out to use the restroom and never returned.

I eased through the huge mansion using ample caution to remain quiet. There were a few hired hands doing their miscellaneous chores, so I nodded a farewell to them, so they would know that I was exiting the premises.

Once I exited, it was just my kind of bad luck. A rainstorm started, and not only was it raining, but the sky was clear and sunny without a rain cloud in sight. It started raining extremely hard, and then hail started slamming against the hood of my Acura Legend. As the storm grew more fierce, I just kept thinking, *good thing I had the windshield wipers repaired the other day.*

Now depending on the traffic, my condo was only fifteen to twenty minutes away from Orange County. Yet no matter the distance, being a black man in a thunderstorm, with a handgun and attached silencer would get me a life sentence in California. So I was real nervous about driving around on parole strapped. Due to being paranoid, everything seemed animated, so to relax, I turned on the heater; but the heat only made the ride a little more uncomfortable. I could tell my nerves were getting the best of me. As I gripped the steering wheel, my hands started to sweat. Suddenly, I could see my condo, so I made a quick turn off of Bloomfield Road into an alley, then made a right turn on Centralia Road, which allowed me to cruise up safely to my home. Man, I was glad somebody kept the security gate open, which allowed me to ease into my parking stall.

Finally, I'm home. Home at last. Home at last, I thought.

CHAPTER   4

The clock on the wall displayed the time as being 11:45A.M. Since it was early, I had to get into something. After the day's ordeal with Capo Dona, I decided to call Lefty Bull to find out what day Eddie's funeral was going to be on. Before calling Lefty, I hid my pistol under some old outdated Los Angeles Times Newspapers.

"Hello?" A female answered.
"Hello. Is Lefty home, this is Vonny?"
"Hold on a second."

My pal Lefty had an obsession for women. It's crazy cause for as long as I've known him, he has always kept different girlfriends by his side. But not your average girl, he was always with the ones who liked other girls. I remember when Eddie was still alive, we'd all clown around about Lefty never having three females in bed at one time. He already had a mad fetish for sleeping with two women, but for some reason it was never three. I held that against him too. To Lefty three women at one time was the ultimate. As I daydreamed, I quickly came to my senses.

"Vonny!" he barked, happy that I called.
"Lefty what's up...?"
"Nothing much," he said in a frustrated tone.
"Say, Man I called cause I needed to find out what day is the homeboys' funeral?"
"His mom is still making arrangements as we speak. She's still in shock, Vonny," he paused. "I can tell she hates my guts for what happened to her son."
"What actually happened, Lefty?" I asked. "Why would she feel that way about you?" I questioned a second time, starting to get angry about this whole situation. "Lefty, she knows the three of us are close."
There was a long pause.
"Vonny, I never told you about what happened because this whole thing is like a bad dream. Man, it's crazy! But the homey Eddie got shot in my coupe," he said full of regret.
Instantly, I started screaming into the phone.

"What the fuck do you mean!"

Although Lefty seemed scared to tell me what happened, I pressed him, and insisted that once and for all, he get down to the bottom of all this.

"Someone blasted him in the head executioner style."

Not only was Eddie a close friend of mine, Lefty was too. But after listening to his story, there were two things that had me at a standstill. One was the fact that I'm on call for a criminal syndicate and at any given time I could be summonsed for my services. Second, was the fact that, I'm also deeply loyal to both of my childhood friends whom I grew up with. So however Lefty decided to handle this situation, I was gon' back him up a hundred percent to avenge our homeboy Eddie.

...Static traveled through the reception of our phone signals.

"Lefty, what happened to Eddie is a done deal, already. Somehow, we both need to get over it. It'll be hard, but time heals wounds," I explained. "What matters now is that we give Eddie a proper burial for his family. By any means don't ruin yourself, feeling like it was all your fault." I told him, trying to keep most of the guilt off his back.

"Stop bumping your gums assuming shit. Mister know it all. I haven't even told you or nobody yet about what happened to us out there."

For some apparent reason I felt frustrated because it seemed to me like Lefty was holding something back.

"Then what happened?" I further questioned, this time raising my voice up a notch.

"Man... Over the telephone?" he stated in a way to let me know that he didn't care to discuss this matter over the phone any longer.

I needed a head change so I went old school and rolled up a blunt. I applied some honey to make it burn slow. Now normally for me, it was rare to be getting high while on parole, but this was a special occasion. Eddie being gone for good was real disturbing for me to deal with at the time, so I had to calm my nerves.

"Vonny." Lefty called my name. "Are you still there?"

"Yeah. I'm still here." Going straight forward with his thoughts, he started talking again.

"Good cause Vonny, - Eddie was set up."

"Now we're getting somewhere," I said, exhaling smoke from my lungs. "Go on!" I pushed, encouraging him to give me more details. I could tell by his procrastination that he didn't really want to relive the incident all over again.

There was a short pause between us.

"I was driving my low-rider, hitting switches, showing out, and clowning around with my car club on Crenshaw Boulevard, when Eddie called me out of the blue. When I noticed it was the homey, I immediately answered. He told me that he knew somebody who was looking into purchasing a thousand pounds of weed."

"Continue…." I said, taking a strong pull on the blunt, letting the smoke exit my mouth and nose extremely slow.

"Well, after he'd mentioned a thousand pounds of weed my antenna's went up. I was like either this is a set up or somebody that we don't know locally, or out of town was down here trying to buy some spices. One of the two was the deal, so I brought my heat." Lefty did have a valid point, I figured, dragging in a small puff. "Vonny, you and I both know that nobody but Five-O buys that much weed in the hood, or anywhere else out here in Los Angeles like that."

"That's a valid point. It's probably the fuckin' feds, Cuzz?" I stated.

"Look. Stop assuming shit all the time. That's why I felt funny about telling you what happened to us." Lefty griped, sounding as if he was about to cry. "I should've known better," he complained.

"Damn right, you should have known better!" I screamed into the phone. "Since I've been locked up these past few years, to me the both of you seemed to have forgotten how things work out here on these streets," I continued, because Lefty needed to be tightened up. I felt real pissed off at both of my friends acts of stupidity.

"Vonny, cutting straight to the point, I fuckin' shot down two undercover plain clothes DEA agents," he fussed back. "Man, I didn't know that they were cops. I just didn't know..."

Then suddenly the line went dead. I immediately called him back. He quickly picked up on the first ring.

"Vonny, they set Eddie up! They set him up with a bogus drug buy out in Long Beach. We were down by some docks," he informed me, "So I just rode with him cause I had to give him two hundred bricks to make up the difference. He was a little short, so he needed a few from me."

Lefty seemed real honest, which is why I started to believe him. I had all I wanted of my honey blunt, so I slowly put it out in the ash tray.

"Lefty, call me back later."

"Cool, and if you're not doing nothing later, stop by my house tonight. It's very important, so come alone," he demanded.

"I'll try to make it around nine or nine-thirty," I said, hanging up.

Whenever Lefty said something was important that was usually a sign. That's one of the reasons I respected him so much, because he was a realist throughout our entire friendship. *Life is real and real things always happen when one neglects the practice of being discreet. Damn, I can't believe Eddie's a body now. Man, ain't that a bitch*, I thought to myself.

A short while later... another call came in. However, between the two calls, the honey on my laced blunt had caused me to zone out, so I was on one of my power naps. Not to mention that I had a shot of Gin, which also contributed to keeping my buzz going. And the fact that I had to get up to attempt to answer that annoying phone, was really not going to be an option at that moment, so I let it ring. After the ringing finally stopped, my nap was ruined, so I was forced to go on and get up.

I pressed the number 2 on the remote, and *Dear Momma*, by the deceased rapper Tupac came blasting out of the speakers. The thoughts of my friend, Eddie, and Tupac helped me realize how blessed I was. *Damn, from my past lifestyle, what happened to both of those cats could have easily happened to me. I'm real blessed* – I thought, sitting on the couch just to reflect over my life.

CHAPTER 5

I was trying to get some rest, but it felt like someone was poking something sharp in my chest. Whatever was going on, I felt very irritated and uncomfortable. And though I thought I was dreaming, it happened again, and again. *I don't remember ever having company over here before I dozed off to sleep*, I thought to myself. *And if this is a robbery or something, did someone steal my ten-G's from the safe already, and are they here to kidnap me?* My mind was playing tricks on me. Whatever the situation was, I never moved to figure it out.

"Vonny wake up, boy!"
That sounds like Capo Dona 's voice, my mind raced.
"Vonny, wake your butt up!" he insisted, shaking me until I was fully awake.

After Capo Dona spoke, I still felt reluctant to open up my eyes. *There goes that pestering poke in my chest once again.*
"Vonny, get up I said! You hear me talking to you."
"I'm up!" I yelled, glancing at the person in front of me with sleepy eyes. Shocked, I had to make an inquiry. "Hey, how did you get in here?" I asked.

Mr. Palmer laughed softly.
"From me Mr. West. Can I collect my rent now, nine-hundred smakeroo's?" he bragged with a hideous bad odor on his breath. When I finally totally came to, my landlord was smiling down over me. He had these ridiculous gold fronts on his teeth, and all the rest of his pearly whites were stained and discolored.

My landlord, Herbert Palmer was a very presumptuous and wealthy man, who wore extravagant jewelry. He had gold everything. You name it, he owned it; and trust me, if I say that gold was his worst downfall, then it was. Mr. Palmer was one of those highly affluent investors whose expertise specialized in the renovation business of old condemned buildings. Some were commercial, others were residential. Almost overnight, he'd become a very wealthy entrepreneur from fixing up old properties and turning them into comfortable urban living environments. Rumor had it that he never sold any of his land.

I jumped up from the sofa unexpectedly.

"Anybody care for a drink?" I asked, feeling as if I had dues to pay or something.

Capo Dona glanced at me surprised.

"I thought you told me that you don't drink, Vonny?"

"I do sip occasionally. Only the good stuff. Besides, I don't drink to get drunk," I said, lighting up an incense.

"I'll have a glass," Mr. Palmer requested, taking a nonchalant glance at his gold Oyster Rolex watch. "Rum and Coke on the rocks, please."

"Mr. Palmer, if somebody was lookin' into buying this condo, how much would you say this home is worth?" I asked, filling his glass.

"He won't sell any of his property," Capo Dona said.

"Mine your business, Boss," I said, walking over to hand my landlord his drink. "It won't cost a dime to stay out of mine," I joked.

Capo Dona smirked.

For some odd apparent reason, Mr. Palmer didn't feel for my affections in buying this piece of property from him. He thought I was playing. *Maybe cash on hand could persuade him*, I thought. *Maybe I should go up the stairs, unlock my safe and pull out $10,000,* constantly raced through my head; *maybe then he'll see that I mean business.* Since I had his $900 for the rent, I downed my glass in one gulp and excused myself. I treaded up the stairs to grab his money out of the safe. While upstairs, I counted out a little extra for later so, I wouldn't have to go back to get more.

On my way back to the stairway, I heard a conversation taking place downstairs between my boss and Mr. Palmer. They were relaxed and enjoying themselves. From the sounds of it, Mr. Palmer was clowning me behind my back about being late every month on paying my rent, and me not having my money every month was beginning to become a big problem. But after listening for a moment, I could see Capo Dona had my back.

Suddenly, their conversation made a drastic change from them discussing me to real estate contracts, and then to Capo Dona wanting in on some major cocaine smuggling business Palmer was involved in. I immediately thought, *Man he clearly knows that it is totally against the conglomerate's law to deal in any kind of drugs.* And from what I overheard, Mr. Palmer wanted my boss to finance $2.5 million dollars for a private jet. He was trying to get Capo to fly drugs from South America to other parts of the world. Capo Dona had suggested that if he was to supply the capital for a new plane, then he was entitled to a 60/40 cash cut once his end of the deal was met. I wanted so bad to trample down the stairs and disrupt the sneaky little rap session, but out of respect for my elders I changed my mind. I wasn't raised to be disrespectful to adults, so being that they were both in an intense negotiable mood, I continued to eavesdrop from the top of the stairway.

Capo Dona was clever. I have to admit that I admired my bosses' negotiation skills, his smart wits, and his ingenious ability to use words that allowed him to manipulate a conversation. He was quite impressive. What impressed me even more was I'd never seen my boss at odds like he was this particular day, and man was he working. *If this is work, then this is the line of work I would prefer to be in,* I smiled.

But Mr. Palmer wasn't buying whatever it was that Capo Dona was selling. He was also a skillful negotiator. Both of them were business tycoons who shared very similar theories that any profit was a good profit. They also both believed that everything in life; especially when it came down to money was to be considered as taking care of business. It was like the two attended the same school or something.

After all that time of dealing with Mr. Palmer, I had no idea that he was ever involved in moving drugs. And though I was listening at that moment, to be truthful, I really didn't care. People got killed nowadays for knowing too much; so I could care less about their side meeting. And when I thought about the fact that I had a couple of wealthy, high-powered gentlemen in my living room, wearing $1,000 Armani suits, and discussing how to transport hundreds of pounds of cocaine and heroin in from South America, I almost wanted to put them out for even bringing that to my spot.

Things were getting serious, and with the new found wisdom of Capo Dona trying to become a big time player in the drug smuggling trade, to go along with his secret partnership outside of the committee, kept me vigilant about the unexpected. Being privy to what was really going on helped me realize that things had just gotten dangerous. I heard all I needed to hear and as I headed back down the stairs all I could think was, *Anything could happen at this point. I was real cautious.*

"Mr. Palmer, here's my rent money for the next two months."

Once I entered the room, they both stopped talking, and glanced at me.

"I promise from now on that I'm going to start making my payments on time. It's just that my money has been funny lately. You know things are kind of slow," I said, assuring him, as I held $2,000 cash in a wad of freshly crisp brand new big faces in my hand.

Instantly, my landlord dug in his attached case to grab his checkbook.

"You know I have to keep up with all payments, Vonny," he said. "...the IRS is a beast."

"I'm hip." Capo Dona followed.

The moment I threw the wad of cash on the coffee table Mr. Palmer snatched it up. He mentioned that he had another business appointment, and then headed towards the front door to excuse himself. My landlord never counted the money or nothing. He just got paid and left. On his way to the door, he did speak to my boss though.

"I'll call you when your capital is needed." Then he was gone.

Capo Dona never gave a response, but that didn't stop me from starting in on my boss.

"Was it a coincidence for you and my landlord to be over here together, like this, at the same time?" I asked, since we were now alone with a little time to talk. He looked at me with mixed emotions, because he knew his cover was blown. "Or was it just one of your bright ideas to use my house as the location to discuss your illegal business?"

I knew I was out of line, so it burned my heart to ask him that. He stood to pour us both the last of the leftover liquor.

"What seems to be the problem?" he asked, looking serious at me. "You're not going to mention this to nobody, right?" It was more of a statement then a question. I sighed deeply, but did not answer. "Right..?" he said a second time.

There was a long pause between us. Still not saying anything, I started to clean and wipe around with a rag.

"Capo Dona, you know your secret is safe with me."

"That's my boy!" he chortled.

"You two scared the shit out of me," I complained. "Nearly gave me a heart attack..Ya'll coming in here waking me up like that."

My boss kept staring at me like something was on his mind.

"Well it's time," he finally said.

"Time for what?"

"It's time for me to enlighten you on the target, how to execute successfully, and neutralize our victim Mobie 'Dique' Lewis," he sighed, sounding amused.

"Meaning?" I prodded, acting as if I was green about the mission.

In this line of work one has to be prepared mentally. Since this was going to be my first contracted killing, I was ready and sort of anxious. My boss smiled at me.

"It's real, Vonny!" he announced. "A good friend of ours that works with Internal Affairs has done his own little investigating, using phone taps, close body trails, money wire traces, and has provided some information as to where our target will be parlaying on December 4th. That information came straight from a confidential informant, and it's somebody we can trust because they are close to him. They are also working for the local authorities in his crew. He's a reliable source, too! So don't get to interested in the outcome that you let your curiosity influence you to stay at the scene. Once the hit is complete, remember what I explained to you before about being able to exit out fast," he sighed again. "The CI helps those who help us, Vonny," he said. "So be careful."

A snitch is a snitch in my book. Crime pays nowadays and I was ready to start making me some good money, and I truly wasn't trying to hear all that shit my boss was preaching right then.

"Where at?" I curiously asked, sitting myself down on the sofa.

"In Las Vegas at the Bell-Trinidad fight. Here's two ring side tickets. From there you can see everything that's going on down there, and around you. You can also mingle around the area with those passes, so get yourself familiar with your surroundings." Capo Dona pulled out two Mandalay Bay Event Center tickets from his coat pocket, and threw them in my lap.. "I told you before that I'd contact you when the job was ready. Are you ready?"

My heart swelled with pride.

"I want to handle this project my way," I boldly opened up.

Capo Dona's voice was cold.

"What do you mean? There's two passes and after all the work I've been putting in, helping you out on this to ensure that things go smoothly, and here you go trying to be defiant against the plan. Vonny, besides, your way will take too long. You don't have any inside connections that could get you close enough to the target."

An aura of tension crept in the room.

"I just don't want nobody holding my hand through my first real paying job, is all."

Capo Dona was heated with the stare of a gangster in his eyes.

"Look! Don't start playing games with me, Vonny. I promised your dad before he passed away that I'd take good care of you and show you the way, raise you in our way of living, the correct way, and I promised I'd teach you how to survive without him." My boss confirmed in a very understanding tone. "You were not picked by choice to be around us. You are one who's fortunate enough to have been born into this familial by blood, son."

Balancing my poise, I stood there mesmerized with that feeling of supreme confidence. It was this kind of fearless feeling that one gets before doing their first shooting.

"I'll do the job your way, boss." I assured him, with anticipation in my heart for a positive outcome.

"Done right!" he reminded me with that same ice cold look. "I'm not going to let you sink this ship, Vonny."

After a few minutes, I thought about what he'd just said.

"Don't worry, man. I got this." I said, guaranteeing him that my loyalty was genuine. The exclusive moment we shared together was very special to me. We both had finally compromised and agreed that I was to stay away from all inner circle involvements, until Mobie "Dique" Lewis was in the mortuary. Out of sight. Out of mind.

CHAPTER 6

The drive all the way to Riverside County was slippery and wet from previous rainstorms. Since my car wasn't winterized, I drove through the streets with caution. It usually takes a few hours for me to drive out to Riverside from Los Angeles County, but today, the wet weather conditions had me running a little late. As I sat behind the steering wheel of my Acura, I couldn't help but think about how good it felt being out of prison. Not to mention the fact that I also had a little cash in my pocket, which was rewarding.

Physically I'm out but mentally I'm not. It's a struggle to stay free out here with all the temptations around. Capo Dona once told me when I was fresh out, that some people will get a shovel to dig with, while people like us got a spoon. His words always make me stronger out here in this Wild West. To be out of the 5 by 12 small cell the feds called my home for five years felt good. There's no question that freedom was a beautiful thing. Lucky for me I only had one celly the entire time I was down. His name was Quincy Simmons. A lot of the older convicts knew of him as "Poppa Q" or "Old Man O."

Mr. Simmons was originally from New York City. He was in his late sixties. He looked good for his age, and I can't even believe how much he would exercise to stay in shape. Every day in the cell, he did lots of push-up's, back-arm's, and sit-ups. He worked out so much that he made me feel guilty whenever I wasn't working out. While on lock down, he would workout at times, too. I even remember during one of our lengthy conversations, him bragging to me about his old flamboyant lifestyle. He shared stories about things he did on the streets many years ago.

Back then I enjoyed those late night talks while drinking coffee and snacking on pastries until the sun came up. Unfortunately, like most of the old school street players from back in the day, he was one who fell victim to the unconstitutional federal laws back in the late 70's. Yet, a lot has changed, and now with life prison sentences, there are numerous denied appeals. As a result of that, the ex-drug kingpin is cut off from society forever, with nothing to look forward to but a lot of inhuman isolated years and institutional lockdowns. My ex-celly is one of the many federal prisoners whose freedom has been taken away over stuff that was allowed once the "Hearsay" rule came into effect. As a result of that, this rule will leave women and men buried alive in prison for the rest of their natural lives. Forever.

Since I had the moon roof open, I'd just so happened to take a quick glance up into the beautiful night sky. While looking into the sky, I thought for a hot second, *Damn it feels good to be out of the feds*, then cruised off of the freeways exit ramp.

Lefty lived in a decent middle class, predominantly all black neighborhood, which was far away from the KKK and their prejudice rift-raft. It was mid-evening when I finally pulled up in front of his driveway. I quickly got out and before walking up to the front door, I rolled me a fat one, lit it up and took one quick hit, before smashing it right back out in the ash tray.

While standing outside, I noticed the air had a crisp, fresh aroma, coming from the back of the house, so that's the direction I headed in. Once I opened the gate, I noticed Lefty going at it. He was barbecuing boneless steaks on the grill. He was there sweating over the grill like someone who worked in a smoke house. He had barbecue sauce everywhere. He even had sauce all over his neck.

From the grill, smoke lingered throughout the yard like a patchy fog, which made it difficult to see. I felt like being mischievous, so I attempted to scare Lefty.

"Freeze!" Instantly Lefty's arm went up.

"Don't be playing like that, Vonny," he responded, all shaken up. He was startled.

Sitting next to the grill was an ice chest fully stacked to the top with Budweiser. We laughed for a moment, and I pulled up a small picnic chair to relax.

"Hard day?" Lefty asked, looking over at me.

"Man, I got a lot on my mind right now. How about you?" I replied, popping the top off my bottle of beer.

Lefty stopped what he was doing to stare at me. When I stood to stretch my body a bit, I caught a glimpse of the steaks and made a request.

"Make mine well done, almost like crispy." I said, gulping down my drink.

"I know how you like your food, homey. I can cook!" he ranted. "And don't get too bent right now. I still have to catch you up to speed on what's going on."

"Lefty what's up, Cuzz?" I questioned, with a faint bit of concern.

He kept his voice low and got straight to the point. "Man, Eddie's death was all messed up the way it went down. It happened so fast, I had to react on instinct. When I saw the homey's body fall to the ground, I had no control over the situation, so there was nothing I could do besides handle my business the best way that I knew how. And for Eddie, Man, I put in some major work."

I made a gesture with my eyes, which caused him to pause. Lefty sighed for a minute.

"One-Time cold blooded ass shot Eddie down right in front of my face!" he explained. "I seen it, Vonny. When the homeboy went down, that's when I came and started chopping them down to pieces with AK-47 bullets."

As I was watching Lefty turn the meat on the grill, a vision of the violent attack came to mind. Immediately, his words paralyzed me for a second.

From the glare in his eyes, I knew he was telling me the truth about this whole ordeal. I could see that his loyalty was heartfelt. And I respected him. Now even though I've been committed into a Black Illuminati by secrecy, I was still willing to go all out for the cause of my childhood friend. Eddie's misfortune had my head screwed up big time.

While one of his hands was rotating the food on the grill, Lefty used his other hand to dig in his pants pocket for a key.

"I'll tell you what. Go up the stairs and look in the bedroom . . . the one on the right."

Holding a new bottle of beer in my hand, I headed up to the room. As I walked down the hallway, I stopped, immediately noticing two very attractive young lady's watching Nip/Tuck on the big screen. The show must of been quite interesting, and I only say that because of all the attention they both were giving the TV screen. From what I could see, the lead actor, Christian had some hot blonde bent over a table pounding her from the back. I gulped down the last of my brew, and then made a right turn, to head towards the room. The girl's never saw me creep past them. From my jeans pocket I pulled out the key and inserted it into the lock; then I opened the door not knowing what to expect. The upper section of the house felt so peaceful and cozy. All of a sudden, I felt sluggishly tired. *I must be drunk,* I thought. *S*ince the room was so dark. I had to feel around for the light switch. When the light was turned on - on the bed were large bricks of cash that had been neatly wrapped in cellophane. Instantly, a feeling of disgust crept up in me.

Damn! Instantly a smile came to my face. My eyes felt like they were going to pop out their sockets, and all I knew was if this was a dream, then I didn't want to be awakened. When I walked around to the other side of the bed, I noticed that Lefty had stacks of brown packages lying neatly on the floor. They were all wrapped and taped tight for some type of delivery with [P] markings all on them. Also, the room reeked of an unpleasant odor of dope and dirty money combined.

"We are definitely rich now, Vonny," Lefty casually stated, standing in the doorway behind me.

"Absolutely..." I replied, looking back over my shoulder.

"Vonny, after I smoked those two cops, the trunk of their car was still open, so that's when I grabbed every and anything that wasn't bolted down. I took all the money out first."

Though my heart knew what we both were into right now was wrong. I was still proud of Lefty.

"That was smart of you to think to take all the cash out first." I told him, sitting on the bed.

Lefty rolled a joint of light-green chronic and lit it.

"You and Eddie both knew that the Man ran the drug trade. After I got popped and sent away to prison, I sent you guy's strict instructions to stay away from dope." I expressed, looking very serious as a result of an experience I don't ever want to relive. When his eyes met mine, I hoped he heard me. "Lefty, drugs are a poor individual's setback."

"It's not our fault that Eddie was conducting business with Five-0. I'm not too fond of having my life in jeopardy like that either, Vonny.

Man, I was just the lookout man, and I ended up knocking down two police officers in the process. Give me a little credit, here."

I had to think. "I do. I do." I said, with a feeling of dishonesty racking my nerves. I was hiding a very important top secret from Lefty. After I had takin' the solid oath of the Black Illuminati, their dark hidden secrets was what I had to live with for the rest of my life. My loyal promise was for me to never reveal myself as having any inside connections with the elite criminal brotherhood to anybody outside our familial.

While feeling displeased with myself, a profound sense of regret crept through my veins like thorns. Because my childhood friend. Lefty had a loyal bond with me, one that could run deeper than the deepest ocean; here I was hiding something from him. Sadly, I was tipsy from all the alcohol I'd been drinking. And to make matters worse, I staggered whenever I tried to walk, and I was sleepy. Then I fell and put the side of my face on the cold floor.

Lefty laughed.

"You're loaded. Man, how you gon' go to sleep at a time like this?"

"Easy! Watch me." I snapped back, rolling over on my back. "I was sipping on some Captain Morgan's earlier today," I said, "..and I feel like I gotta throw up."

"Well don't do it in here. Vonny, go lay down in the guest room," he suggested. "I'll have one of the girl's bring you up a plate. Man, you probably need some food on your stomach."

***

When I finally opened my eyes, it seemed like I'd been sleep for a long time. And by the time I regained consciousness from the thunder nap, all the lights were off, the house was quiet, and I was still lying on the same pile of money that I'd been lying on from earlier. My brain felt clogged with pain, and my head thumped from the pounding of a vicious headache. And my body that was in such good shape felt extremely exhausted. Oddly, I was still able to stumble to the restroom to wash up and brush my teeth. So after getting rejuvenated and regaining my composure, I walked to the guest bedroom, which across the hall and turned on the light. There on the dressing table was a healthy plate of barbecue ribs, drenched in lots of sauce, along with all the other necessities, and a tall glass of home squeezed lemonade.

Suddenly, I noticed a female lying over on the waterbed. She was laying there in a deep sleep, so I didn't disturb her. The open invitation to fun would have to wait. Instead, I seemed to be more hungry than anything, so I invited myself to those delicious ribs.

There I sat totally devouring the sides that were left. There was potato salad, pork-n-beans, and corn on the cob. While nibbling away, the female began to yarn, but I ignored her. Well, I ignored her until she got irritated with my moving around and handed me a paper towel to wipe off my face and hands with.

"Here take this. You just over there making a mess," I heard her annoyingly complain, insisting that I take the towel from her. "Here," she suggested again, only this time reaching to help me out. She took her hand and dabbed the sauce from my lower chin.

"Good looking out," I stated, politely asking her a question. "Umm - What race are you?"

She laughed at my question.

"I'm black," she replied, smiling at the confused look on my face. "I'm mixed. My dad's black and my mom is Asian."

Her smile was warm and friendly, and whenever she smiled, it just kind of lit up the room.

The clock on the wall read fifteen past two. After pigging out on all of my food, I had to admit that food hit the spot, and I was full. My stomach was so full, I decided to just lay back on the soft bed and get to know this pretty little dime-piece that was sitting next to me. Without my asking, she bent down and simply took off my shoes.

"Thank you, that feels so good," I softly commented. It was something very different about the way she made me feel. As she worked on my feet, I noticed she knew how to treat a man. *Yeah, this girl was heaven-sent,* I thought. She looked up at me smiling.

"Now - that's better. You feel better," she asked.

"Sure do. Thanks," I quickly stated, marveling over her beauty.

To me she was flawless, with nice round perky breast that had nipples that stood at attention. She was pure sexy, and for a while we laid side by side with one another, laughing and talking for what seemed like hours. Then, our conversation heated up, and before I knew it, I was making the first move.

"Excuse me, but do all Asian girls sleep with no clothes on?"

I mean I'd just finished doing like five years in prison, so I was just curious. Her eyes calmly scanned my body, so I could tell she was assessing me.

"No, I don't believe they do, but I do," she said with this sensual look in her eyes. "And I told you that I'm black," she laughed.

With those slanted sexy eyes of hers, I couldn't hold back my thoughts of how pretty she was. Her beauty was remarkably different from any other woman I'd ever been with before, which is why I found myself feeling very lucky to even be lying next to her. And from the looks of it, she seemed to think everything I said was funny, but I couldn't even get mad at that, because the way she was looking at me with those eyes had me in a trance. I felt sort'a like a kid under a magical spell.

As a result of us becoming quite comfortable with one another, we eventually stepped up to more intense measures while in bed. She was relaxing, and snuggled up under my armpit. It was almost as if we both knew each other for a long time. There we were kicked back, hugging, kissing, and affectionately touching on each other. And though there was no penetration, I sort of felt like we were already being quite intimate. By her sex drive being so alive, this allowed me to suckle and play with her soft breast.

She rubbed her soft hands across my chest, and from the way she outlined my tattoo's, I was instantly aroused. She had that special touch that I'd longed for and desired for so many years. However, while embraced between her breast, I never made it known that I had been in the feds. That was my business, and I preferred to keep it that way. Suddenly, she lifted her finger and started to play with my navel. As she circled it with the most tender touch, she kissed my belly with her soft lips. I noticed that she looked at my face for a response, but I was so gone that I had a slight hard on, which she'd noticed poking through my pants. I guess that's what inspired her to unzip my 501's.

Without wasting any time, she slowly reached inside my open zipper, felt around for a few seconds, pulling my dick out and started to passionately kiss only the tip. She licked it like a Popsicle, causing it to be very slick from her saliva. Before I knew it, her lips were stretched wide around my core, then she held the tip for a few seconds between her soft lips, allowing me to pulsate in her mouth.

Out of nowhere, she took a deep breath, nodded her head, then her lips easily slid down, completely covering me. Quickly and with much force, she plunged so far down over my love muscle with her moist mouth that the tip of it touched the very back of her throat. She gagged, and so I jerked myself from her attack. The pleasure for me was excruciating, but I still reinserted my dick back into her mouth and jabbed it up against the back of her throat with force.

"Take your time!" I explained, massaging her breast gently with the palm of my hand.

Her nipples were hard, almost like tiny pebbles. As her eyes met with mine, it was then that she became woman and I her man. From experience, she simply began to suction the ache away that was building up deep within my groin. Most of it came from the intensity of our passion. The suction squeezed tighter and tighter over my erection, aware of the fact that I was about to explode in her mouth, she stopped and started massaging my family jewels with her fingertips to ease the tension. With full pouty lips, she looked up at me.

"Not right now, please not right now!" she begged. So because I was excited, and so was she, I popped out of her moist mouth to calm down.

Since this girl was in total control of the situation, I just sat there relaxed. And she continued, I eased back to enjoy watching her lips do what they were doing. I grabbed the back of her head with both hands, and without me asking, she nodded back down over my shaft to let my tip touch the back of her throat again. This time I pushed down a little harder, and she held me deep up in her mouth. I struggled with myself to keep from cumming. Yet, again from experience, she took another deep breath and forced me further down into the inner walls of her tonsils.

Over and over, faster and faster, she rammed her deep throat, letting me run with ecstasy through her mouth cavity. I was about to explode in her mouth, but somehow I resisted having convulsions instead.

Then, it happened unexpectedly. I tensed up while still firmly holding the back of her head. Instead of pulling away, she bobbed up and down on my shaft, allowing me to empty myself. The more I fed, the more she swallowed, totally devouring my flavor with her expertise. When those sexy eyes of hers looked at me with supreme confidence, she smiled with a devilish grin. As she flirtatiously bit on her bottom lip, she let me know her expectations for the night.

"Before you leave, I want you to fuck me from the back," she boldly expressed, crawling towards me on her hands and knees.

In one motion she laid her head on the pillow, gapped her legs wide open, and entirely exposed herself to me. I wasn't totally spent yet, but as my manhood eased deep inside of her, she grimaced a sigh of relief. She wanted me to pound her from the back, so that's exactly what I did. I rammed her hard and good, just like she told me to. I continuously plunged as far in as I could possibly go, deep into her plump juicy channel. And quitting was not an option because this went on until the early morning daybreak.

We were two sexually active Trojans, clashing together in combat, sweatin', grindin', passionately kissin', and making real hard love until one of us submitted. She whoever she was had just given me the best fellatio I'd ever had. Her head was the bomb. And as we both laid side by side, drenched in sweat, her eyes met mine.

"We out did ourselves," I mentioned, breathing hard.

She reached under the bed for her purse to get a Newport. *Damn, I know she ain't about to go there cause I hate women who smoke*. To me that was a total turn off. Sensing that I was moody, she glanced at me and put her cigarette out. That's when I popped the big question.

"So, what's your name?"

"Soul," she laughed.

"Soul?" I asked. "As in soul-mate?"

"No just, Soul," she replied. "And yours?"

"Vonny West," I answered, looking into her eyes. "But you can call me Vonny."

"Vonny, do all the girls get this treatment?" Soul's voice was flat and dry. I gave her a gesture with my eyes, then a gentle squeeze.

"I found my soul-mate." I smiled, realizing she was trying to stroke my ego.

Now for me morning sex was the best, so after our little talk, we ended up making passionate love again and again. Being that Soul was the best I'd ever had, made me even more attracted to her. After a hot forty-five minutes of mind blowing sex, I was sore down between my legs. Finally, it was over, so we dozed off together in our own private thoughts.

***

"Rise and shine, it's a beautiful day!" Lefty said, barging through the door. Soul and I were still asleep and holding each other.

"Man, we're sleep!" I shouted, throwing the covers over our naked bodies.

"Vonny, get up! It's already ten o'clock," he said. "We have business to attend to."

"Me and Soul still sleep!" I shouted, motioning with my hand for him to leave us alone.

Besides, she felt so good, I didn't want her to move. Without any more discussion, I signaled for Lefty to get out. As he walked out the door, I was too tired to move that's when I slipped back behind my dime-piece. Plus, Soul had drained all the life out of me, so it felt good being with her. *This is just too good to be true*, I thought to myself, falling back to sleep.

CHAPTER 7

The Black Illuminati is nationally respected. They also have a strong deeply committed relationship with an influential inner circle of Dons. I truly believe that we should get a cut off of the money Lefty stumbled across. That's only to let the others know that he is somehow gang related. If not, then the Pit-Bull Mafia, one of California's secret and most treacherous organized crime families will arrange for Lefty's assassination. Since they're mostly the financial backbone of Hollywood anyway, it'll sort of be like a protection pay off, and legitimate of course.

My underworld associates will surely back me up on this one, being that the undercover cops were corrupt. I was in my feelings about this whole ordeal with Eddie and Lefty because those police officers were scheming off of drug profits, and then they sabotaged my homeboy. Eddie got smoked from trusting his connection. And Lefty is rich from keeping it real with a friend. While I on the other hand, since being a part of an elite commission, get to sit back, respect, and enjoy all of the loyal altruism around me.

Feeling like it was up to me to try to protect Lefty was a job all by itself. I wanted to make sure that he survived long enough to spend his new found treasure, but if he thought that more drama wasn't going to come from this dirty money, then he had another thing coming. Now, I'll give it my very best, nothing but the best for Lefty's survival, but we all knew that business was business in these fast California streets.

Soul was finally up and getting herself ready, while I, on the other hand, was laid there on the bed, in my own world, trying to think things out clearly. She had just gotten out of the bathtub, was drying out her hair with a towel over her head, and walking around in my T-shirt, with nothing on underneath. The movie Life was playing on the flat screen, she sat down to watch it. From a quick glimpse, I caught her tanned thighs sitting Indian style. Her breasts were full, nipples stiff in an upward position, and rubbing against the shirt. A lotion fragrance from Victoria's Secrets gave off a floral scent. The room smelled just like it too. After one whiff, I decided that it was time to get out of bed and start my day.

She turned, deeply staring into my eyes. As I stretched, I winked at her.

"Good morning, Soul," I bluntly said, slipping into my jeans.

"It is, isn't it?" She replied.

I walked over to the window to open the shade. One can always tell what type a day lays ahead by the weather outside, especially out in California.

"Looks like it still wants to rain," I murmured between a yawn.

"Isn't it so romantic," she chanted, walking over to where I was standing. She affectionately wrapped her arms around my waist, and kissed the back of my neck. "Vonny, making love in the rain is so romantic."

Soul's squeeze was tight, she smelled so good, and as her damp head rested firmly against my back, I imagined making love all over again. As her warm body pressed against my bare back, I could feel the lumps of soft breasts.

I unexpectedly turned around to look deeply into those slanted, sexy eyes of hers.

"Let me go check on Lefty," I eased out of her grip, kissing her on the forehead. Soul's fingers crept down the front of my pants. Instantly, I tensed up because of soreness.

"He's been in that room across from us all morning. The door has been closed, and Ginger cooked breakfast," she expressed, lying her head against my shoulder. I assumed Ginger was the other pretty little dime-piece that was sitting on the sofa next to Soul the night before.

"Hold up, while I go check up on Lefty Bull. Sweetheart, why don't you go make me a plate. And while you're at it, let Ginger know that I do appreciate the breakfast," I instructed, with a tender peck on her cheek. I could tell Soul tried to arouse me on purpose. I think she was ready to do it again, but reluctantly released my manhood.

"Sure, no problem. Whatever you say, Babe."

Soul turned in a slow provocative manner. While still wearing only my shirt, I noticed how elegant her walk was. Her tanned legs were settled high on the tips of her toes, and she had that perfect models poise. She stood up straight, classy chin up posture, with a sashay that demanded attention whenever she walked. Before she made it to the door, I snuck up behind her and slapped her lightly on the ass. I know I shocked her, but I couldn't pass up the chance to give that soft butt a friendly love tap.

"Stop boy!" she quickly snapped, followed with grin and a devilish look from her eyes.

On the way out of the room, I watched as Soul trotted down the stairs. And from the back. I ain't gon' lie, those wide hips looked so good to me.

Outside of Lefty's door, it sounded like snapping and ripping noises. At first I thought paper was being crumbled up behind the door, so without' knocking, I barged in the room unannounced.

"What's up, Cuzz!"

Lefty ignored me. At the time of my unexpected entry, he had dope everywhere, and all over everything. Lefty was looking like a Freemason, stacking bricks on top of bricks. Instead, the only difference is that these bricks were not concrete, these were uncut kilo's of raw cocaine. I mean in the purest form. What the noise turned out to be was him meticulously ripping the brown paper off of each packaged brick. Then he was neatly and very carefully stacking each one on top of the other. And a few he would throw over in a corner to make it all chalky and soft. Dope was everywhere.

"Here, let me help you," I insisted, trying to show some favor.

Lefty stared wearily at me.

"Hey, hold up! Look over there in the closet and separate mine from yours. I don't want your hands touching nothin' right now," he fussed. "Vonny, you're on parole. So I need you out here with me right now."

Using a blue bandana, I tied it around my neck to cover my nose from the bad stench.

"How much ya-yo are we talking about, here?" I was curious.

His eyes glanced over at me and gave me a calm more settled appraisal.

"Four-hundred kilo's of pure cocaine." After his reply, Lefty's smile was full of confidence. As he bragged, he started sweating, so using the back of his hand, he wiped his forehead off and continued to rip open, and stack in a consistent rhythm. I listened to my homey, and made sure I did not touch any ya-yo. I walked over to the closet, stretched my arms out, and then my back popped. I felt a little nervous about not knowing what to expect when the door opened.

"Dee-zaam!" my tone was loud. I felt totally amazed once I saw a heap of money stacked in one huge bundle.

For a quick second, this unexpected good fortune enslaved me mentally. I was emotionally confused as to how fast my life had taken such a drastic turn from rags to riches, and in such a short period of time.

"Don't just stare at it, count it up!" Lefty insisted, handing me a money counter. "Put all the hundreds together first," he suggested. "You should get around two-hundred-fifty grand. Vonny, half of that money is yours," he said, smiling. "We will split everything in half. Fifty-fifty!"

"How much should be in a stack?" I curiously asked, still kind'a nervous.

He stared at me, then sighed.

"It should be around ten grand in each stack," he answered with a sense of uncertainty. "Now, leave me alone. I need to finish counting up all this dope."

This was my first time ever using a money counting machine. I counted $125,050 grand two times. *Now I know what Scarface felt like,* I smiled, enjoying my second count. Lefty ignored me. He was acting all brand new. All of a sudden he was acting like he was - like that.

"What do you want me to do with your half of the money?" I asked, loading my share in a Cambridge sports bag that I'd found in the closet.

"Just leave it in the closet."

I had a slight hangover. After placing my money in the sports bag, I had to lay down on the bed, so I used the bag as a head rest. As I watched Lefty repackage all of the dope in his own plastic wrappings, my mind wasn't there. I quietly watched him, while at the same time, I tried to develop a strategic plan on how we were going to get rid of the cocaine. One has to share a passion for this business, because selling drugs is frightening, and sadly, there's no longer honor and loyalty in that trade. It takes a lot of patience and time, with one constantly looking over your shoulder 24 hours a day from informers, snitches, possible police, and the jackers. The people who have a passion to rob dope dealers. When you're in the game, those streets move fast around you. That's why one may never notice someone who's out to get them. You become their prey, and they can't wait to snitch you out to the local authorities.

This is why I have to be the one out of the two of us to act as the brain of this detail. I guess because this had to happen, is why our so called dope dealing homeboy is pushing up daisies. Lefty was always the muscle in our crew, I've always been the brain, but unfortunately, nowadays, I have other obligations of more importance to pursue.

As I laid there in deep thought, my belly growled. I was starving, so I got up, opened the door and yelled for Soul to bring me my plate.

"Don't call her up here, yet!" Lefty snapped. "The girl's don't have a clue that all this money and dope is in this house. Vonny, we have over a million dollars in assets up here," he complained, sounding businesswise.

"But I'm hungry. And Soul said she'd make me up a plate. That was nearly an hour ago?"

"Not up here."

Soul glanced up at the top of the staircase at me. In her hands was my plate of breakfast.

"Sweetheart, let me help." I politely said, quickly closing the door and running down the stairs to get the plate. "Thank you, Sweetheart," I said, giving her a quick morning kiss.

She smiled with sensitive eyes. "No problem, Vonny," she said, turning to return to the kitchen.

Again, I couldn't help but to stare at those wide hips as she sashayed around. When I walked back in the room I noticed Lefty was almost finished with only a few more kilo's to wrap, "You ate breakfast yet?" I asked and started to eat my meal.

"Yeah! I ate already." Lefty replied. "Is the food good?" he asked.

Soul had brought me a very healthy serving of soft mouth watering pancakes, scrambled eggs with cheese, like my grandma use to make, perfectly cooked grits, and a side dish of thin, sliced crispy, bacon. My pancakes had maple flavored syrup on them. As I ate, I was standing point, with my plate of food on the dresser. I didn't mind, because I was actually comfortable with eating and standing. It was a behavior I picked up while in prison.

Back when I was in federal prison, for hours, we would take turns standing "on point" to watch for the police. We usually did this while someone sharpened knives. Sometimes it would take days, maybe even a week to get the tip to a fine sharp point.

"These pancakes are good," I complimented. I ate everything on my plate, and once I finished, I noticed that trash was everywhere. *This place is a mess,* I thought.

"Where did you meet these broads at?" I asked, rubbing my full belly.

"They work in the club."

"You still work in that bar?" I asked concerned.

"Gentleman's hang out. Anyways, not anymore."

"What do you mean?"

"Like I told you before. If I ever got rich, I'm not going back to work, especially if I could buy the bar. And own it, Vonny!" he seriously expressed.

"Listen to me Lefty, you have to think about what you're doing. Think, Lefty. . . Think!" I protested in a cold tone.

"Nowadays Man, if I got over a million dollars, I don't gotta work for nobody," he expressed with his voice getting heavy.

He does have a point, "...but listen to me!" I said, staring him directly between his eyes, as I grabbed the front of his shirt to let him know that I meant business. "You are gonna continue doing your same living routine as normal. No playing around, you hear me," I fussed, wanting him to see I was serious. "Lefty, this is more serious than you think. I guess you must want the feds to start crawling around, asking questions." He tried to say something, but before he said anything, I blatantly shouted at him. "Homey, you can't just quit your job!"

Now he had something to think about.

"I hear you, Vonny. Now let go of my shirt."

Lefty was mad and forcefully pulled away from my grip. With wrinkles in his shirt, he finished repackaging the drugs, and afterwards I helped out with the trash.

"What should we do with all of this paper with cocaine residue on it?" I asked, before making a careless mistake. Cause I knew putting paper with residue on it in the dumpster for someone to stumble across would have alerted people to our narcotic involvement, and then back to the penitentiary I go.

"I have an idea," Lefty configured. "I'll burn the trash," he casually stated.

"Where at?"

"In the barbecue pit. Where else?" Lefty was so sure that his scheme was a good one and would work. We gave each other five, because I was down with him.

"Well let's do it then," I bluntly replied, holding one of two large Hefty garbage bags full of the pieces of paper. All had ya-yo crumbs stuck to them, too. Outdoors the clouds were lurid and reflected rain showers. "Lefty, it might rain today."

When we finished up, Lefty and I headed downstairs to hang out with the girl's.

"Now you can meet my girlfriend Ginger," he stated, trampling down the stairs.

We got our own thing now. Our own illegal enterprise going on now, so now we can freelance a little, I figured. I don't know about Lefty, but I felt lavishly rich at the time. Now all we had to do was operate secretly. If we could get the drugs to the street as discreetly as possible, without a soul knowing who was behind it, we were about to change our finances like never before.

We swiftly moved at our own pace to the room where the girls were. I shot a quick glance at them, as they leisurely practiced a sexy dance step. They were humping the air, gyrating, and moving their thick wide hips side to side. Some slow jazz song was on and incense were burning, which made the ambience exotic. Lefty and I joined in. He positioned himself to dance with Ginger. I moved behind Soul, positioning myself right up on her hips. That way we would both sway with the rhythm, while I was holding onto her tiny waist. We danced in a slow, love making grind. After the song was over, our spontaneity ignited, causing the four of us to make a decision to have a fish-fry later on.

But first, the two young ladies had to get themselves dressed. They had to get all pretty for us. While they did that, that was our time to make our move to burn the trash. We moved quickly up the stairs, snatching up all the Hefty bags. In less than five-minutes the pit was so full that we had to rig it shut.

As Lefty prepared to burn the bags, I stood there quietly looking on, and rolled a fat joint. I lit it, took a hit, and then passed it to Lefty so he could hit it too. Afterwards, he lit the fire in the pit. In the beginning the flame started off very dim and slow, but then all of a sudden the blaze flared up. I smelled the cocaine being burned, so I put the joint out.

The odor of cocaine as it blended with the paper smelled like a high sophisticated grade of refined paper being burned. The smoke smothered us out, so we retrieved back inside, trying to keep an eye on the smog of smoke from the kitchen window. Lefty opened the cabinet and grabbed a fifth bottle of Hennessey. He poured the warm cognac in two glasses. Since this was hard liquor, I needed a few ice cubes in mine. I was silent, waiting on him to speak. Then I sighed.

"A toast, Vonny!" he said, raising his arm with a glass of cognac half full.

"A toast?" I inquired. "..for what?"

"Yeah that's right a toast," he stared at me.

My arm was up like his. With both of our glasses half full, we made them delicately touch in a salute. I let the strong drink wet my lips.

"To longevity in the drug business!" he said, pleased with our silent agreement.

I quickly raised my glass again, but only this time to tap his. "Salute!" We harmonized together. That moment was one of those L.A. Confidential agreements, not formal, but heartfelt between two loyal friends in the game. For us, things had just gotten as serious as it was going to get for the moment anyway, and the sky was certainly the limit.

You see Lefty and I are not drug dealer's, we jack'um for a living. That's why we both feel strange and out of place about all this dope dealing crap. Out of our trio, Eddie was the one who sold all the drugs. On that note, I felt awkward.

"Lefty, we need to just hide the weight for awhile, bury it away somewhere in your back yard to only bring it up for air when the time is right," I suggested, pouring myself another shot of Hennessey. "When the heat cools off and profits are greater, then we can put the dope on the streets." There was a silent moment between us. Lefty took the joint from earlier and lit it.

"You mean like bringing it up for air later, like in a dry season?" he hit the joint once, and then smashed it back in the ash tray. Lefty turned to me, with no smile and appeared to be unpleased after thinking about my comment.

I nodded, because Eddie had also taught us that time and a little patience was a great asset. To him, it wasn't about how much drugs one had, but instead how much patience and time they possessed, because dope sells itself in due time. From a glimpse I noticed that the clock on the microwave read 1:59P.M.

The fight out in Vegas was only a few days away. I took another sip and went to relax on the leather sofa. Lefty retreated back up the stairs to hide the ya-yo in the attic until it was safe to execute our plan. After all our talk and activity, there was a change of plans for that fish fry we'd planned to have with the girls. I knew they were going to be disappointed, because they were so excited about having one.

Feeling exhausted, I laid my head back on the sofa. I had a head change after drinking Cognac. For some reason, I had a nervous giddy feeling inside because I had so much going on in my life at the time. I guess that is why I was always thinking about how to be invincible in this drug business. I mean, after going to federal prison and now being on parole, my only other biggest fear was the Don's. See, cause in the back of my mind, I knew that the crime bosses could not ever find out about my cocaine business. That knowledge alone would kill them softly inside, and hurt everybody's feelings.

Truthfully, this mission that I'm assigned to do this week is going to be my very first contract job. I've never taken a life before, so I'm scared. The job Mobie "Dique" Lewis was a cold piece of work back in the penitentiary, a bad actor, and cursed like a sailor. Will he resist and try to fight or what? During a jury trial, the man testified in an open public courtroom. He got on the stand in court to testify against several major underworld crime players. Our contacts revealed that he is still to this day, assisting the government and getting people arrested under the 5K1 RULE. He is providing classified information on different gang related families that are scattered in different parts of the United States, and unfortunately some out of the country.

Even right now today, he's still on federal contract, working undercover. That's how the government works once a snitch, always a snitch. They can use a person on any trial testimony for up to ten long years, then after using you up, they feed you over to the wolves. Sometimes they even terminate the agreement informants sign. These subjects are deemed rats, which make them targets that are marked as being expendable.

The only thing that I'm truly worried about is that my first job is going to allow me to get away smoothly with everything. There is no doubt that I won't get my man, because he has to die. Actually, it's over for him, and a crying shame that one has to go meet death's iron curtain as a rat.

To me, a rat is a low down dirty scumbag. Most rats snitch for jealousy reasons, some do it because it simply runs in their family. Others tell for more personal reasons or because of the pressure to inform about what they know. Most do it out of the love for money; which is why this murder is a top choice hit, which also gives the Don's the utmost respect among all underworld associates and their predecessors.

Once I finished my drink and found the joint I was smoking in the ash tray, I lit it. I was honored to be the one who's called as the underling up for promotion under the order. *If I screwed this job up, it'll cost us our reputation for a high priced pay off*, I thought to myself, letting smoke hold deep inside my lungs. Everybody is depending on me for this one, so I couldn't get excited nor make the slightest mistake.

Ginger walked down the stairs, wearing a leopard full body suit. She and I were the only two in the den. As her eyes stared into mine, she appeared to be eager to hit the joint. I slowly passed the joint over to her, and then she started in with questions.

"Vonny, why are you down here by yourself?" she asked, standing over me with a nice plump V between her thighs.

"Thinking to myself," I replied, hoping she didn't notice me looking between her legs.

Ginger was full and thick. The body suit she wore showed every curve imaginable to man. And without a doubt, I saw exactly why Lefty was so attracted to her. The girl was dark chocolate and gorgeous with an extremely smooth sparkling skin from the olive oil she applied, and had dazzling grayish, light brown eyes. I noticed that her fingers were well groomed, and very jazzy looking. I walked over to the window and stood next to her to watch the rain showers outside. The rain lasted a few seconds then stopped. She turned to stare at me again.

"Where is your homeboy?" she asked, and then walked lightly over to the stereo system in the corner. A rap song by Drake was playing softly through the bass speaker's.

"Is he upstairs?" Ginger asked, searching around for the remote.

"Yeah," I answered. "You know it."

She spoke with a formal proper tone, and her manners were polite.

"Do you mind if I turn on the TV for a while?" she requested with a cute accent, while grabbing the remote off the floor.

I glanced over to a small coffee table and there sat a novel entitled, 'Redemption' by Stanley "Tookie" Williams. It caught my interest, so I quickly picked it up and started reading. Not long after reading Chapter One did Soul come sashaying down to the room we were in. She was barefooted, and was wearing a short-short black mini-dress. She made a pivot twist, showing me her red G-string panties, and then sat that soft fat ass on my lap. She then confiscated my glass off the table and gulped down the last swig, which drained the glass empty.

The strong drink made her close her eyes together tight. Ginger who was looking on was sitting on the floor.

"That's what you get, girl!"

"Here." Soul simply said, holding the empty glass in her hand for me to get it from her.

"Don't hand it to me," I told her, blocking her with my arm.

"Silly, it's yours," she laughed. Soul teased, being funny and wanting to play.

Up on the second floor, Lefty was doing a lot of bumping around. Once it sounded as if he fell, because the crash vibrated the entire ceiling, making the ceiling fan swing a little. The three of us all stared upward. Ginger turned the TV volume up and the stereo off.

"Look!" she shouted. "Rodney King just died!"

There on the television was a brief news broadcast that was live at the scene of the late Rodney King's home.

"Rodney King was famous for the 1991 L.A.P.D. beating that was caught on tape is dead today. It was the beating and subsequent acquittal of those officers that led to riots in Los Angeles in the early nineties and also his famous, 'Can We All Just Get Along' phrase, that is what we'll remember most about him."

Another segment followed that story which was live in San Francisco.

"A pimp was shot and killed for pimping a couple's young teenage daughter. She was a working prostitute for her pimp who was found dead in an alley behind an office building in a dumpster. The couple now faces murder charges for allegedly killing their daughter's pimp. More news at five..."

I got up off the sofa to fix me another drink and rolled a fat joint. As I smoked, the news reported another murder that occurred out in Long Beach. Two undercover D.E.A. agents were the main focus in the story. The killer is still at large and has a $100,000 bounty on anyone with information.

"Look the killers are still out there!" Soul exclaimed.

I was silent for a moment as I stared at both Ginger and Soul.

"Fuck'um!" I replied, with a serious expression and no remorse.

Lefty also made Breaking News, regarding all the money the authorities had lost in that deal gone wrong, was upstairs in a room so close to us. *This is conspiracy at its best,* I thought to myself, smiling at the girls who were all traumatized about what was going on in their community. And the fact that only Lefty and I knew about the money law enforcement officials would never get back, made things even more ironic, so much so that I couldn't help but feel a since of self-pride.

Besides whatever was said on the news, only one person knew what actually took place out in Long Beach. And that one person was upstairs loading his attic up with the dope. The girls and I listened with boredom and watched as the news broadcaster kept repeating the same news - over and over. She also made several fraudulent remarks to the viewers of the general public about how the crime occurred. After a few more reports, the police suddenly made an arrest. On live television they showed various officers involved in arresting a bum who had salt-and-pepper cornrows and was wearing filthy clothes. After he was handcuffed from behind, they placed him in the back of a squad car.

A different broadcaster came on relating how insidious the crime was and compared the beggar to a John Billington. After assuring the media that the vagabond was not a suspect, but yet that they were just taking him down for questioning, a caption flashed over the background of John Billington, who was this countries first murderer in the early 1600's.

Outdoors a thunderous rain storm started. I personally had become fed up with all the gloomy news, so I rose to my feet very tight-lipped and fist balled. From my side view, I caught a glimpse of the girls who were angrily staring at me. In not less than a second, Ginger, sitting Indian style, on a Persian rug, took the remote and switched the channel to B.E.T. Next to the fireplace, Soul was smoking on the same joint from earlier, and after one additional hit, she threw the roach between the old burnt logs.

"Looks like that kills our fish-fry," Ginger casually mentioned.

Soul walked over next to me and gave my arm a desirable hug. She looked up into my eyes, as I started rubbing my fingers through her soft wet curls. Her body felt warm and soft by my side, but my mind wasn't into Soul like that at the time. I was more focused on calling my grandmother's house to see if my parole agent called.

"Vonny, let's make a fire," she said softly.

Her suggesting that we warm up the den was a good idea, so I stood up.

"Excuse me, Ginger," I said. As she moved so I could step past her. I was trying to load the last bits of scrap wood in the fireplace. "Where does Lefty keep the firewood?" I asked, searching around for more logs to burn.

"Inside the garage, over in the corner, by the side door," Ginger instructed, as her and Soul both pointed.

This home was new and freshly built not even a full year ago. And since I'd only been over to Lefty's place twice, I wasn't too familiar with where things were. Lefty always kept things neat and clean, *much cleaner than my crib*, I thought, walking down the hallway to the garage. Because it was quiet, and pitch-black, I slowly opened the door. The hinges squeaked, so I was more cautious as I felt around for the light switch.

My other lifestyle weighed heavily on my mind, so it was time to start concentrating more on my mission. First impressions usually are most important, and after Mobie was dead, the body count was going to start adding up. So from here on out, I'd legally and officially be a paid assassin for this syndicate thing I'm up under, but I was not quite a full fledge underground criminal; yet it was time for me to start thinking like one. But I could not just think like normal. I had to start thinking like I was the best in this entire line of business. I had to calculate moves and operate with a plan. Though I had no executive capabilities, I've now graduated into the big league, which is why it was my time to think accordingly. This was my time to shine.

Lefty stepped in.
"Vonny, what in the world are you in here doing?" he skeptically asked. "The girls are waiting on you to fix the fire for them."
"I'm down here thinking, Homey." I seriously stated.

"Man well snap out of it, and bring the wood on up here!" he seemed urgent. "When I came down from upstairs looking for you, I asked the girls where you were. They said you were in the garage getting some firewood, then all of a sudden, I find you in here staring at the wall. You alright?"

"Yeah. I was gone for a minute, I do have to admit." I laughed.

Lefty quizzically stared at me. I guess he was wondering what was on my mind, but he knew not to ask. Some things just weren't his business, and I respected him for that. His eyes steadily met mine with anticipation in them.

"Say Lefty, check this out," my voice was low in a confident tone. "You wann'a ride out to Vegas with me this weekend?"

"For what?" he asked.

He had his nerve to question my gangster like that. After all that was going on, Lefty knew damn well that he needed to get out of the city.

"I got two front row tickets to the Bell-Trinidad fight for this weekend. Besides, you need to get as far away as possible from Los Angeles at least until things cool down a little."

He looked puzzled for words.

"You know that Eddie's funeral is this weekend."

"No!" I responded. "I didn't know that."

Following my response, I grabbed ten heavy logs from the pile to bring into the house. Lefty followed close behind me with a few logs in one hand. With the other hand, he locked the garage door behind us. Stumbling through the hallway, we didn't say a word to one another. We knew from past experiences that in life everything always worked itself out. Our main goal was not to panic. That old outlaw proverb is one I learned while doing time behind the walls. After stutter stepping and carrying bundles of heavy logs, Lefty dropped his load on the floor, while I sat mine down extremely careful so that Soul could admire my strength.

Her eyes darted towards my back as if I was her hero, or something; so I showed off. Immediately, I noticed that while we were in the garage, the girls had transferred the den into a romantic dwelling place for us to kick it in. They had put scented candles everywhere, which made the ambience cozy. While smiling, I noticed a Monopoly game was set up for the four of us to play as well.

"I'm the hat!" Lefty shouted, walking over to the fireplace to flip the logs.

"I could care less," Ginger uttered, counting out fake Monopoly money, and acting like she was big time. "Oh, yeah! We ordered pizza you two," she said.

Soul planted her lips softly on mine for a kiss. *This girl is something else,* I thought to myself, appreciatively studying her.

"I already picked that piece, Homey. Pick another one," I said.

In unison the two young ladies and I agreed to wait for Lefty to get the fire started before beginning our game. Ginger and Soul both knew how to shoot dice, so they both started a fictitious game of craps, using funny game money as if it was a wad of real cash.

"Bet $500!" Soul yelled, throwing down an orange $500 note on the board.

I of course felt a sense of comfort, being that we all started enjoying ourselves. The four of us kicked it, as I held on to the fact that it was my deepest darkest secret that they were playing board games with a real thug. *Yep, I am what I am, and that's an assassin for an elite group that is under the radar, called the Black Illuminati.* As the flames flared up and burned higher and higher, the mood was cozy.

"The fireplace is showing out," I teased.

Lefty, who was all engaged in the moment, rolled up a joint and lit it. I looked over at him in deep thought then from the night before; I remembered that Soul's cell phone was on a charger.

"May I use your phone for a sec?" I asked. "I have a very important call to make."

"Sure, Vonny - Sweetheart. But first give me another kiss," she puckered her lips with her eyes closed. The smell of bubble gum lingered in the air, so I planted one right on her mouth.

"Thank you," she said smiling at me.

"Don't mention it my dear." I sarcastically stated, standing to my feet to head up the stairs for some privacy. Soul was defiantly on my mind as I exited the room. Ever since I'd exposed her to my realness, she'd just smiled, giggled, and laughed at any and everything I did or said. Her bubble gum flavor wet gloss stuck on my lips, so much so that I could nearly taste the smell. That alone made me grin a little. *Was this a sign of being sprung on a female?* I asked myself.

Soul's cell phone was a girly pink with a matching charger. I had to admit that I really liked the girl. She was sexy to me. I could tell she wasn't a busy person either, because her phone hadn't rang all day, which was cool with me. While holding the phone, which smelled like in my hand, I caught myself snooping. I pushed the redial button, and a green censor light beeped on and off. The little bitch was smart. She wasn't like most clumsy females out here in the game. Soul's game was tight, and I admired that flaming hot trait about her, as well as her provocative sexuality. *This bitch can suck a mean dick,* I thought to myself.

"A yo, Lefty!" I roared, standing at the top of the stairs. He didn't answer, but I could also smell weed being smoked. So after a few seconds, I shouted from the top of my lungs once again. "Leeefty!"

"Yooooh!" he screamed back.

"What's the number to Eddie's mother's house!"

"Say Vonny, the pizza is here!" he yelled back. "Three-one-zero, seven-seven-four, eight-zero-three-three!"

I scribbled the number down on an old outdated Buttman magazine as fast as I could. But before calling, I decided to first call over to the parole office to check in. I needed to see if he wanted me to come in since it was Monday afternoon. I thought of a reasonable alibi, just in case he wanted to see me immediately. As I was tapping in the number, I felt like a kid all over again. It was like reporting in to my mom. I also felt degraded about reporting in to another grown ass man; especially so that he could be sure I was out here being a good boy in society.

After five rings, a receptionist finally picked up. She answered in shrewd Jamaican accent.

"Parole Department! Mr. Glass' office."

"Yes, is Mr. Glass in today?" I asked, trying to seem extra polite. "This is Vonny West calling to report in for the week."

"I'm sorry Mr. West, but all clientele caseload's are excused for two weeks, or at least until after the holidays."

I looked at the phone as if she'd just told me a joke or maybe what she said was even a set up.

"Meaning?" I questioned, mesmerized from what I'd just heard. There was a silence between us.

"He'll contact you to let you know when to come in," she stated. "Happy holidays!"

"You too." I said, eager to get off the phone. "Be sure you let him know I called."

"Sure will Mr. West. And have a nice day."

After hanging up, I called Eddie's mother's house. A recorded message connected, indicating that it was a disconnected number. Feeling disappointed or maybe after dialing the wrong number, I tried it again, but got the same response. Being that I'm a go-getter, I decided that I'll try back later. While holding the phone in my hand, I nervously anticipated calling the Don and them, but knew not to.

Capo Dona was to me a true living godfather. He and the other crime bosses gave me goose bumps whenever I was around them. My boss would not have had a favorable day, if I called him godfather. I could just see him now, telling me that I watched too many movies.

"I'm not in or a part of no snitch ass Mafia!" So whenever he was around, I never called him godfather. The last thing in the world I ever wanted to do is disrespect any of the Don's. Most people who did are not still around to speak on it from their lack of showing disrespect in the past. I was silently thinking for a moment. After erasing my business calls off Soul's phone, I placed the pink thing back on its charger, then headed back down the stairs to go chill with my friends. *Well at least I didn't have to report to my parole officer for awhile*, I thought on the way back downstairs.

That gave me more than enough cushion to handle my personal business. Time is an important asset; especially if one uses it correctly. Out of the blue, I returned to the den unannounced. I looked down at the Monopoly board, glanced at both girlfriends, and then at my homeboy. Suddenly, a smile crept upon my face. Here is where I wanted to be. This was my foundation.

"Vonny, come over here," Soul said, eagerly looking forward to my company. "Here, sit with me. Your pizza is getting cold."

Lefty Bull started pouring us all drinks.

"I already know, Vonny. You want yours on the rocks."

I was silent for a few seconds, just staring, and then I walked over to sit in between Soul's thick soft thighs.

"Here is where I need to be." I mentioned softly.

"Sure-is!" Soul said, quickly nuzzling my neck.

CHAPTER 8

The warmth from the fireplace provided a cozy atmosphere down in the den. Hot flames snapped from the fire as it crackled and popped behind us. The four of us enjoyed ourselves, and we ate pizza until we were full. Unable to avoid the temptation, we also drank the last of the cognac from earlier, and topped it off with some of that good weed Lefty Bull had growing in his back yard. Usually I didn't smoke on spices that were home grown, but this time I made exceptions.

Usher could be heard softly singing throughout speakers in the den, *"I'm in my drop top, cruising the streets. I gott'a pretty-pretty-pretty, pretty thang sitting next to meeee, yeah! I pulled over..."* Soul with a envious smirk on her face was staring me down.

"What?" I snapped, smashing the roach down in an ash tray. She did not reply right away, but I could feel her deep stare right on my ear. So I asked, "Soul what is it?"

"I hope you took care of business up there?" Her dark brown eyes had jealousy in them somewhere. "What bitch did you call?" she asked, frowning. I wasn't about to play that game, so I looked at Soul with a serious expression on my face.

"Soul, don't start. Please."

She was silent and shrewdly just stared back at me. Now, all of her ghetto behavior was coming out, which she earlier tried to hide. They say that, you really get to know a person after being around them for so long. I'd just met Soul, and was surprised as to how she was acting already. From her attitude I figured to myself that I'd better back off a little. I shouldn't have sexed her up like that, giving her all my love in one night. Next time things were going to be different. Instead I'm going to take it nice and slow with her. One of the rules of being made is not to get too emotionally attached to a girl or girlfriend, but wives and personal whores were different. What I've learned is that most whores do become wives. For situations like that there was an emotional gap that needed-no-explanation. I met Soul in one night, and on that same night, it was wonderful, but under my criminal culture I had a big responsibility and one of them was not to get seriously involved with a new girlfriend. Besides, she was too close to Lefty. If my personal business happened to leak out, in any way, I'm done.

A cold smile crept on my face.

"Come here babe and kiss me," I said, noticing she just wanted to be held.

She rested her head on my shoulder, then looked up into my eyes.

"Vonny, whenever I'm around you, you just make me feel so good," her voice was soft and sincere. "You feel so good, Babe."

Truth be told. Soul wasn't ready to be held down by the stress that came along with my line of work, nor the lifestyle that I live right now. So, feeling something in my heart for her, I just held her close to me and felt no regret inside. It was what it was. And that's just how the rules were handed down, and there was nothing that could be done about it.

From a quick glimpse, I caught Ginger was smiling at the both of us.

"You two, y'all need to stop all that hugging and kissing," she stated, turning to look at Lefty. "And for the record, you guys owe us this quality time anyway."

"You want another drink?" Soul asked, softly letting go of me to sashay over to the table to pour us all more drinks. Like always, from the back view her soft fat ass was looking good. I grabbed the dice, shook'um in my fist and threw a nine. Next, Ginger slid a three. After Ginger, Lefty rolled an eight. Soul rushed over and unfolded a clumsy seven.

"You first, Vonny," Ginger said, gesturing with her eyes for me to roll.

Everybody's eyes eagerly looked down for my point as I slid a double six.

"That's my baby!" Soul exploded, moving the solid gold ocean yacht forward twelve spaces for me.

I was excited too, but there is one thing I never do when I'm around top of the line gorgeous women; and that's lose my cool. To argue in front of the girls over the derby hat was useless, so I let Lefty have the hat before one of us got mad. That's one of the tiny mistakes a lot of guy's make when they are in the presence of pretty females.

My old celly, Poppa "Q" used to say back in the penitentiary, "A woman will make you or break you down softly if you let her. She has a certain power that GOD gives her over a man. She's sharp like an ice pick and she knows how to chip small pieces from a man, until there's nothing left inside of him. Always be the man and stay on top of the game.

From the very beginning, the game is theirs, so refrain from arguments. Arguing is for females, men take care of business. It's called good old fashion politicking. If one was to find himself in a silly argument, then that person was not on top of the situation of things, so maybe he should check himself before he wrecks his respect."

I had rolled a double the first time, so I rolled again. This time I let Soul roll. She smelled so good, with her jet black curls tightly pulled in a ponytail. Her firm breast sat high on her rib cage, exposing way too much cleavage. So, out of respect, I pulled her back against me.

"Snake eyes!" she shrieked, unaware that one of her titties was nearly hanging out.

"One more double then you go to jail, Vonny," Ginger gently hinted.

Souls body was pressed close against mine, but I was still able to pick up the dice.

"Don't remind me," I said, making the dice hit a nine.

Soul picked up the yacht to do the honors. After my small spotlight of glory; Lefty Bull rolled next; then Soul; and Ginger pulled up the rear. We enjoyed playing Monopoly until late in the evening. As a matter of fact, we ended up losing track of time. That's when we all decided to add some spice to the game, and play some strip Monopoly. All four of us were drunk, so it didn't matter how the game went. We all agreed that whoever landed on another player's motel or property with four or more houses on it would take off a piece of clothing.

This went on for hours. Finally, the clock over the fireplace read eleven o'clock. It was getting late and I had to get up early in the morning, so I wrapped up our game.

"Okay… enough is enough," I said, standing to my feet to hide my number one stunner, which was stiff as a log down there. Once concealed, I took my sweetheart by her arm to leave.

Soul glanced between my legs and seductively rolled her tongue around her lips.

"Let's call it a night, Vonny."

We both held each other's hand and I trailed close behind her as she headed up the stairs. From behind me, I heard Lefty softly ask Ginger to look in the cabinet for a comforter. The fireplace logs were dim, almost like they were fighting to stay lit. But they didn't care, because they were going to campout down in the den for the night.

The door to the room was closed so I opened it. I watched as Soul slowly eased the door shut behind her. I looked into her eyes because I started getting hard. Before I knew it, she stripped butt naked all the way down to her shaved V between her legs, walked over to me and unzipped my pants. As her eyes had lust in them she smiled, tenderly biting down on her bottom lip. My desire to kiss, forced me to pull her closer to me. Soul pulled back, and held my stiff dick in her hand. As she rubbed my hard shaft, she eased down to her knees. Standing directly in front of my penis, she grabbed the tip and was forced to talk.

"I love the taste of your nut, Vonny."

Without a word, I grabbed the back of her head to guide her face and mouth toward my penis. She sucked my manhood, moving her mouth up and down, and around and around, letting the tip jab on the insides of her jaws. As I released my seed of warm cum down her throat her mouth was like a vacuum. Soul used both hands to hold each of my thighs. As she swallowed, she looked up at me and stood to her feet. Still holding my glistened organ in one hand, she turned around and rubbed the tip between her asshole, and then pulled me until I shot again right in her nice tight butt.

Finally, I thought it was over, but she bent over my rod to let me cum in her face once again. While she tasted the tip with her tongue, I was exhausted from being completely drained, so I leaned back up against a pillow, and relaxed my head. From what I could remember, the way she made love to me was a passionate luxury. I had fun riding her curves. Actually, I was so lost in the ecstasy that I never wanted it to end.

After what felt like a quick nap, I woke up in the wee hours of the morning with Soul lying on my chest fast asleep. I had a slight headache from last night's drinking, and the odor of sex lingered in the room. I knew that play time was over, but I had that same smell of pussy all over my face. So knowing that I had things to do, I decided to get up and start the day. It was time to take care of business, yet my playmate didn't think so. Soul had me rapped in a romantic hold, which made it difficult for me to free myself. Slowly I eased her arm up the best I could, and then slid myself from under her naked body.

"Where are you going?" she asked, puckering for me to kiss her. Her eyes were still shut. "You were awesome last night. Vonny, when you're around me, I feel like you can make me do anything."

I stared at her then kissed her, quickly.

"Good morning to you too, Soul," I said, "Sweetheart, give me a second and I'll be back." I said, kissing her forehead.

I walked around the house while everybody else was still sleeping. It was quiet, except for the two lovers' down in the den who had a snoring competition going on. I walked over to the big picture window to take in the view, immediately noticing that the sun had burned its way through the rain clouds. Since I had some thinking to do, I only allowed that to distract me for a brief moment. Seconds later I strolled over to the kitchen to put on a pot of coffee. It's funny, but ever since I was a kid, early mornings always seemed like a good time to concentrate; especially when things were nice and quiet. That time alone was an excellent time for me to analyze and strategically come up with a plan.

The main problem I had was trying to figure out how much money to give Eddie's mother for his funeral, or any other unexpected expenses. I also figured that she would need to buy herself a new home somewhere nice or at least in a location where busting a cap wasn't a fundamental thing to do for youth in the hood. I came up with the idea to give her about $100,000 in cash, which would leave me with $25,000 to put in my safe back at home. For some strange reason a feeling of ill regret crept inside me. I needed to give Ms. Banks more, but I was just getting on my feet myself, so I needed some money too.

After the coffee was ready, I quickly downed my first cup, and then poured another to take back upstairs. I opened the door to the room that the sports bag was located in. It looked as though it had been untouched, but just to be sure I unzipped it. When I peeked inside, the money appeared to all be there. It was still banded together, so I zipped it back up and tossed it over my shoulder, and headed across the hall where Soul was.

Since she slept nude, I couldn't help but notice that one of her thick wide hips was exposed. It was hanging out of the sheet, and I was getting turned on again.

"I brought you up some coffee," I softly said, not sure she was awake.

"You're leaving?" she asked as her head rose from the pillow.

"Yeah. Baby girl, I gotta go." I nodded, sipping on the mud.

"I don't drink coffee, Vonny," she grumbled.

I put the cup of mud on a night stand next to the bed, then let go of the bag.

"I'll miss you, Soul."

"Well, let me give you something to think about while we're apart," she smiled.

She had the same urgent sexual desires I had, so I unzipped my 501's and started gently caressing the tip of my penis. She looked at my expression, and made a whining noise as she yanked and pulled on my buckle. My sexual appetite was craving her, so I helped her hands pull my pants completely off, and eased her close to me.

"Morning sex is the best," she whispered, kneeling down. Soul grabbed my manhood, and jammed the head of it so far in the back of her throat, I damn near gagged myself. She was deep throating my dick with expertise, so my voice went flat.

"Soul, the door is still open. Let me go close it before someone walks in on us?"

I informed her of our situation, but that didn't stop her from choking and sucking on my dick. The pleasure was excruciating, and she drove me crazy with the way her soft tongue rolled around on the tip of my love pole like a porn star. Then she started sucking harder and harder, which caused a faster rhythm. At the moment of climax, she bobbed her head up and down, slow and long on my shaft, until I started to cum in her mouth.

Her eyes got big as she spit me out of her mouth to allow me to shoot out on her face. Next thing I noticed, she was holding my spent organ in her hand, laughing at me. She bent down and slopped off the rest of the semen that was covering the tip. I felt as if my body was floating from my soul. I do admit, Soul's head game was the bomb, and again she had given me some of the best head I'd ever encountered.

After she was done performing, I had to lay back on the pillow for a few minutes. I was totally exhausted as my playmate dosed back off to sleep. That's when I got up to take a hot shower.

CHAPTER 9

Before taking the long and boring drive out to Los Angeles, County, out of routine, I glanced at the gas gauge. It was on empty, so I drove into the nearest Shell gas station. The sports bag was tucked safely under the front passenger's seat, right next to a Tec-9 that I'd grabbed from Lefty Bull's house. He didn't know that I took the gun he had under the mattress, but I grabbed it when I snatched up the bag of money, and I made a mental note to myself that I'd have to call him later to let him know I had his heat.

Unexpectedly, a greasy service worker with dingy black hair walked up to the car, using an orange rag to dry off his hands.

"Nice car!" he said. "What can I do for ya today, Mr. Acura Legend?"

He smiled, trying to be funny and showing off a rotten front tooth. That tooth had so much decay on it that it was dark brown. He also had a bad body odor that wreaked an unpleasant smell, which was so disgusting that I gagged a little. On an empty stomach, the smell nearly made me vomit. I killed the motor, and went from there.

"Fill it up!"

"Will that be cash or charge, Sir?" he asked with bad breath.

I sighed, then looked at him.

"Cash."

The radio was playing Jazz. I loved Jazz and while looking around for my new Kendrick Lamar's CD to put on, I started to bob my head to a Braxton Brothers cut. As the gas pump clicked, the station worker peeped his head out from under the hood. As he closed it, he smiled, and then wiped his hands off on that same rag from earlier.

"Sir, your oil's fine. That will cost you exactly forty-five dollars!" he said, speaking over all the noise outside. Around us, traffic was moving full steam ahead, so I handed him a $50.00 bill and moved on.

"You, keep the change," I told him, slowly pulling out of the gas station's parking lot. As I tried to merge into the morning traffic, a motorcycle race between two knuckleheads caused me to swerve. A feeling of relief came over me once I cruised onto the I-91 freeway ramp. The windows in my car held in the bass from the 15-inch woofers in my trunk. Moving along the interstate at a rapid 75 MPH on this beautiful southern California day made the long boring ride more comfortable. The sun was up and the sky was light blue. There was not a rain cloud in sight, so I didn't have to rush. I set the cruise control on 70, and let my speed stay there my entire trip to Cerritos. I glanced at the clock, and the time was 11:15A.M. when I rolled across the wooden bridge at the entrance gate to my condo. Somebody had left the gate open, so I just cruised on in, making sure to close it back with my remote. I made it to my parking stall, only to notice that my Ducati was untouched. And in all honesty, it felt good to have finally made it home safely with the money bag. As I put the gear in park, I felt a sense of relief.

Before stepping out of the car, I grabbed the sports bag from under the seat, shoved the Tec-9 in it as well and got out of the car. Calmly I walked to my front door, checking the mailbox on the way. I heard music blasting, so quickly I rushed to unlock the door and walked in. With my hand inside the bag, and a finger on the trigger, I looked around for any intruders. As I listened to 92.3 THE BEAT, it played its normal everyday R&B repetitious reruns. An oldskool jam was on, so I turned the volume down just a little.

Daddy was home now, so without any delay I anxiously ran up the stairs with my new found treasure; but before getting comfortable, I had to check my phone for messages. There were two waiting. The first one was from Tameka. She was my ex-girlfriend who played way too many games with me. I didn't know why I even put up with so much of her bullshit. It might be because she's so fine and resembled the singer Aaliyah so much. I listened to her soft voice on the message and smiled.

"Vonny, Sweetheart, could you at least call me sometimes. Call me back as soon as you get in!" she demanded, and then the line went dead.

I stared at the machine for the next message. Capo Dona's butler, Dexter's voice came on. He was speaking in a confidential and very intellectual tone.

"Excuse me Sir for calling your home in such an untimely fashion. Mr. West, I do admit that it is so unprofessional on my part, Sir, but if you will, please forgive my manners. Please be informed that Madam Miranda has requested your presence at supper with us this evening. A car will arrive at your residence around 21:00 hours to pick you up. Please be ready. Good day, Mr. West."

"END OF MESSAGE!" the machine chirped.

That was my call. It was time for me to go to work. My home provided not just a place to lay my head, but a low-key hideout as well as a place I could operate on orders that were highly classified until the night of the hit. This is how the business of the elite black secret society works, and it is conducted in such a secret way to avoid a criminal prosecution that people in today's society have never seen before.

I went into the bathroom to take a long piss. When I came out, I went to the safe and put all the money away, allowing the door to remain open. I opened the bedroom window, so a breeze could come in. After inhaling a few refreshing breathes, I turned and quickly bent down on one knee to count out $100,000. As I organized my money, I put all the $100 C-notes in $10,000 bundles, then loaded the banded cash back into the same Cambridge sports bag. The rest went back into the safe.

***

The ride out to South Central gave me enough time alone to think. Eddie's mom was such a sweet and loving person, and from being around her for so long, I knew she could really use the money; especially the $100,000, during such troublesome times as these. *Damn, I'm gon' make her instantly rich over night. And how can I tell her the real story about where all this money came from? I can't,* I thought. *Besides, Ms. Banks is religious, so her Christian values and morals will not allow her to accept it from me, and I don't want to put her on some guilt trip, knowing that she really shouldn't take the money, though she needs it.* If I knew her like I thought, I knew her pride would get in the way. So I decided not to tell her. *I figured I'll just make up some kind of peace offering story for her*, I thought, exiting the 105 FWY onto the Harbor 110 FWY ramp.

When I was a young kid out playing in the old neighborhood, there was a night game we played when the streetlights flicked on. All the hood kids called it, "Doorbell Ditch." The game was fun, because one of the homies would creep up to a house, any house in the hood and ring the doorbell, while the rest of us hid behind a bush or somewhere secluded to watch. The occupants of the residence would emerge at the door, most of the time opening it, to find nobody there. That just happen to occur because whoever's turn it was to ring the doorbell had already ran like a bat out of hell to safety.

We were dead up in the hood, so it wasn't never any love lost with our neighbors. From that little game back then, most of the youth on our block gained some of our little gang confidence. We became evil, fearless little criminals in home invasions throughout our youthful years. Nowadays it's the other way around. Instead of me home invading, I'm home delivering, but for a good solid cause. I made a smooth right turn on Eddie's mother street at a easy 10 MPH speed, passing by the small stucco plastered home. As I did, my eyes started to sting with tears. I didn't want her to see me like this. Out of the crew, I'd always been the emotionally strong one; so instead of going right to her house, I decided to cruise on through the Broadway Gangster's hood to see what my old friend Sugar Bear was up to. Before I dropped off the money, *'Summer Vacation'* an old song by Ice Cube was knockin' extremely loud through the bass speakers. So, I turned the music down a little to respect my surroundings.

While I was doing fed time at The Poc and the homie, Sugar Bear and I did four-years on the same unit together. Bear was from Broadway Gee's, a predominantly laid back hood in the South Central gang infested area. For some reason, I never got into the street gang thing. And even though I knew a lot of people from Juvenile Hall up to the Federal Prison system, all the gang banger's knew that I was neutral. Growing up, I'd dealt with the Crips and Bloods, but truly only affiliated with the kidnappers, bank robbers, and jackers. I'd seen a lot and been through a lot growing up in the ghetto streets of Los Angeles. After my mother died, I mainly considered myself as an average kid who adapted to his rough living conditions.

As I cruised through Broadway's hood, looking for Sugar Bear, I noticed just like in Compton, everybody had on the color blue. Blue bandanas were worn around all the young people's heads; blue sneakers, blue hats, and blue pants and shirts. There was no doubt, that the dress code in this particular hood was blue.

'Down Home Blues,' is the motto among the Crips.

When I pulled up, the homie Sugar Bear was out in the front yard. His shirt was off, and his chubby body was all exposed. He was messing around in the trunk of a Low-rider, when out of the blue I pulled up to the curve unannounced. He didn't notice me driving up in my Acura, so I rolled down the window. Around here in this area I was considered a high-roller with a car like mine. But, if they only knew the car was stolen. My car was a tagged vehicle.

"Bear!" I shouted, putting my keys in my front shirt pocket, and without warning, I noticed guns being pointed at me.

"Bear, what's up with him?" a young loc'ed out Crip asked.

A female Criplette came from around the house with a SKS semi-automatic machine gun aimed at my chest. The entire gang was curious about me being in their neighborhood. Bear came to my rescue. Walking in my direction, he had a blue bandana on his head that was tied towards the front.

"Kick back! This is Vonny, my friend from the Pen," he said, shaking my hand in a brotherly fashion.

"What's up, Bear?"

From a glimpse, I caught one of the little loc'ed out Crip's messing around with one of those new bop-guns. Capo Dona had one disguised as a pen, but theirs was disguised as a cell phone. I was silent for a moment, as I thought, *the hood is something else.*

"So Vonny, what brings you around here?" Bear asked.

Seconds later, gun shots sounded off, sending all of us to the ground for cover. The youngster with the SKS went gun-ho like O-Dogg from Menace II Society, but her shots were of no comparison.

"I'm hit! I'm hit!" Somebody screamed.

The fact that I was on parole was the only thing circulating in my mind. I was in a state of shock and panic. At the time, I was disarrayed. Sugar Bear got to his feet, pulling my arm for me to get up in the process.

"Vonny, get out of here. Man, it's on around here! And you don't need to be around here!" he yelled, throwing a couple of cell phone guns on the front seat of my car. "Homie, the instructions are inside the box." I was hesitant to put the key in the ignition. "Now get the hell out of here before you get caught up!" he yelled, causing me to quickly drive away.

Bear didn't have to worry about me being in that area, because I wasn't trying to go back to prison. In fact, who tries to really go to prison? My clothes were all muddy from lying on the ground, so right after that, my main goal was to get over to Ms. Banks house, drop off her money, and get back on I-91 East back to Cerritos. Besides I had an appointment later on that was more important than being nearly shot to death out in South Central.

Coincidentally, while waiting at a red light was the same Chevy station wagon that had just been involved in the drive-by shooting, was right next to me. I sat tight-lipped and angry as hell, as I thought, *Those are the same fool's that just tried to kill me.* As I glanced over, I noticed that one was female. It didn't matter though, because they were going to get the business for the stunt they'd just pulled. In my stash spot was the old ancient pistol my boss blessed me with. I was told only to use it when need be, and right now was one of those moments. Without a second thought, I eased it out of the stash real slowly and turned the music off. Then scanned my area before placing the burner on my lap to see how many rounds were in the chamber. I rolled down all four windows to look the five occupants' in the eye. All stared my way, and the desire to kill was in their faces.

Capo Dona always told me to look a man right in the face before you take his life, so patiently I sat, and sat, and sat. Once the light turned green, I aimed the .38 Special directly at the driver's head, and squeezed the trigger. After being fed all six bullets to the dome, he died instantly. In broad day light blood and skull fragments were all over the inside of the vehicle, slowly the Chevy station wagon eased forward in a creep. Before I drove off, I noticed that the driver had fallen over in the female's lap who was riding shotgun.

There was no way possible that the surviving thugs could blast back at me, nor catch me, because their driver was dead in the driver's seat. Their crew got caught slippin', and as a result of that, their driver was now nothing more than a lifeless corpse that had just been murdered by a virgin assassin. I felt a rush of adrenalin crawl up my spine. *Damn, I got skills at this killing thing, so from here on out I think I would prefer to live my vicious lifestyle as a ghost. I am now a member of an elite class of people. The rules for engagement from my deepest fears has now been changed. There's no turning back to ever being normal again.*

Finally, I made it to Ms. Banks' house. Up until a few moments, I felt a nervous tension; one that was actually so thick I could taste its mental pressure. When I parked in front of her house it looked real quiet. All of her guests were obviously gone, so before walking up to the front door, I took the muddy shirt I was wearing off, and left it in the car. So at this point, I was only wearing a white wife-beater. I grabbed the sports bag that was full of the money then I shoved the gun in my front pocket for easy access. I noticed a head peeping from behind some bright peach colored curtains. As I knocked on the door, it quickly flew open.

"Vonny?" she said, looking surprised. "Vonny, is that you?" Ms. Banks quickly hugged me tightly. Her embrace was warm and motherly. "Well don't just stand out there, come on in before you get yourself shot. These fool's have been shooting around here quite a bit lately," she warned, holding open the screen door for me to enter.

Immediately, I walked in and went directly to the restroom to wash up. I placed the sports bag on the bottom shelf inside of the linen closet, as I smiled at the thought of Eddie's mom appearing to have picked up a few pounds in the shoulders and stomach area. I hadn't been over to see Ms. Banks in five or six months, but she still looked good for her age. She seemed to have more gray streaks, and I could see that her hair was starting to thin in the middle. She was usually always so happy and full of life, yet today I noticed that she looked stressed out and worried. The old lady didn't know that I knew about the financial arrangement she had with her son. Before Eddie died, he decided she couldn't work any longer, so he took care of her, the bills around her house, her mortgage, and paid off any debts she had. She knew these expenses were all being paid for from his drug money, but it was what it was.

As I entered the kitchen, Ms. Banks hung the phone back up on the wall receiver. Her dark, thick hands were covered in flour; it looked like she was making some kind of homemade biscuit dough.

"Vonny, you still like dumplings?" she asked, hard at work. I nodded yes in response to her question. "Oh, and how is your grandmother doing these days?"

"She's fine."

There was a moment of silence between us.

"What's in that bag you brought in?" she asked, stirring a pot of chicken stew.

I lifted my head to look at her.

"It's a surprise from me and Lefty, Mom."

"A surprise?" she quickly asked, still working the pot.

While looking at her, my heart bled regarding her loss, so I snuck up behind her and kissed her warm cheek.

"Yeah, that's right. I put the bag in the bathroom. You can look in it later. But right now, I'm starving, what' cha got good in here to eat?" I asked, opening the refrigerator to look for some food. Ms. Banks always kept goodies in the box.

"Boy sit down at the table and let me make you a hot plate of these chicken and dumplings," she insisted. "… and take yourself a plate of them for later on."

I sat down at the table to let her serve me. I didn't want to be rude, but truthfully I had to get my car out of the hood. The ghetto bird was up flying around, and after that killing at the light, I'm sure the police were searching for a suspect to arrest. Ms. Banks turned around from the stove, holding my plate of food. The mouth watering honey corn bread was already on the table. It was smelling good and had butter dripping off the sides.

"Before you drove up, did you hear all that shooting going on out there?" she asked, rinsing off her hands in the sink.

I nodded while grubbing down on her good old fashion soul food. From outside, an ambulance could be heard speeding down the street. It was doing at least 65 MPH in a residential area. Ms. Banks sat at the table restless, watching me enjoy her cooking. I reached for her soft hands.

"The food's good."

"Well, earlier I had company over. Then after hearing all those gun shots, they just ran off," she smiled at me. "God knows I need to leave this neighborhood for good and settle myself down somewhere nice. I just keep praying, Lord, please send me an angel!" she said. "Vonny, where are you staying these days?"

"Cerritos."

Ms. Banks watched as I sopped up the last bits of gravy on my plate with one of her corn bread muffins.

"Now that's a nice area." She smiled and took a napkin to dab at the corners of my mouth. I stared at her like a son would. With as much as I wanted to stick around and talk to her, I couldn't. She didn't know, but I knew I was the one that the police was out there looking for.

"Yeah, it is," I stretched. "Well, Ms. Banks, I have to get going before all the streets get blocked off."

"I know Baby; I know. You take care out there," she stood at the same time as me. I stared with deep concern into her watery eyes. Soon tears ran down her face. "Stay a soldier, Baby," she whispered in my ear. "That's the only way it seems like you're gonna be able to survive out here. Before Eddie got himself killed, I wish I could've told him those same words."

"Yes, Ma'am," I said. "And thanks for everything."

"I'll call your grandmother to let her know what day the funeral is going to be, as well as the exact location...!" she yelled, smiling from the porch as I was getting into my car.

I sat behind the wood grain steering wheel, tightly gripping it. While angry about this whole situation, I still felt good about myself and had a sense of peace about my old friend Eddie. At any minute, I knew Ms. Banks was going to peep in that bag and find all that money. I'm sure that one-hundred grand in cash was more money than she'd ever had at one time in her entire life.

On my way to the freeway ramp, I'd forgotten to stick the dirty .38 back in the stash spot, so I drove with caution. There was also the fact that two new lethal weapons disguised as cell phones were lying on my backseat as well, so at that point, I had to pull over and properly put things back in order; especially before heading out to Orange County. On my way home, I smoked a joint of light-green weed before stopping in Compton to give G-Momma the extra plate Ms. Banks had sent.

After leaving there, I headed out to Capo Dona's. When I finally made it to the Dana Point area, the joint was nearly gone. While listening to my favorite Reggae band, Steel Pulse, I cruised up the long cobble-stone road and parked directly in front of the huge double doors to the Castle. Dexter immediately stepped out.

"Good day, Mr. West," he said, decked out in his black Versace suit, and speaking just as formal as ever with that proper English tone of his. Whenever I was around Dexter, I always got a kick out of the way he pronounced his words.

"Who's here?" I asked, getting out of my car.

"Just me, Lady Miranda and the usual help, Sir," he nodded, closing the car door for me after I stepped away from my vehicle. As I followed the chief butler through the elaborate grounds, I noticed that Dexter was wearing his ice white gloves, with his polished wing tip Stacey Adams. The shoes had a special shine to them, one that stood out. Also, his suit and collar was heavily starched with a light gray silk foulard neatly in place around his neck.

"What's the occasion?" I asked, trailing closely behind him.

Dexter disregarded my question.

"Master Dona laid down strict rules for you to remain put until he calls."

"Dexter, if you don't mine me asking, where is the boss?"

"He's in the air, Sir," he turned to me and said with a serious dignified look on his face, and his chin held high.

"In the air!" I repeated.

"In the Lear jet, Sir."

I simply went along with the flow of things. If that was the order then who was I to buck the Boss. After all I am a secret Plant, who was planted in this organization to carry out all secret classified orders for the crime bosses. Our family is mostly centered around trust and loyalty, so with an allegiance only to ourselves, that's where my loyalty lies. In an obscured nonchalant way, I slowly made it down by the pool area and decided to relax in the Jacuzzi. I had this blood oath thing on my mind and the life I'd just taken back in L.A. was weighing on me, so I had to think and relax for a few before Capo Dona called.

Dexter trailed my every move, so once I got out of my clothes, he neatly folded everything I took off, treating me like royalty. The warm whirlpool bubbles were so refreshing that they relaxed me. The water felt good, too. It was not too hot, nor was it too cold. Actually, it was just right, so I laid my head back, and just chilled. It almost felt as if someone was looking at me, so I opened my eyes to see Dexter still standing behind me with my clothes draped over his arm. It was as if he was protecting me from something.

"Hit the massage cycle?" I casually asked, taking advantage of all the special attention. As I relaxed, I noticed Money News was reporting that the company Caterpillar, Inc. had topped its fifty second week high, at $114.00 a share, which led the NYSE total stock listings at 32%. That sparked my attention.

"Ahh... Dexter, can you bring me the phone, please?" he looked down at me. "I wanna call my broker."

"Well that would not be appropriate, Mr. West."

I rose waist high in the water.

"I got stock in that company!"

"You have rules that you must follow, Mr. West. If you do not, then there are consequences for your actions," he said simply.

Me being me, I went with the flow of things and sat back down in the water. Dexter adjusted the massage cycle to high, resembling the ambiance of a steamy tropical rain forest. Out of the blue, Miranda showed up at the pool area unannounced.

"It's getting late, so are you staying the night?" Miranda inquired, holding in her hand Capo Dona's private phone.

"No. I'm just waiting for your dad to call me." I never glanced up at her.

"Here he's on the phone now," she stated. After handing me the phone, Miranda walked over to the windows and closed all the blinds. She gave Dexter a sly look. "Dexter leave us alone, please."

I put one hand over the receiver to block out any sound, then questioned Capo's daughter. "Miranda what the hell are you doing?" I whispered.

This girl is a mess, I thought, watching her pull off the white terry cloth robe she was wearing with absolutely nothing underneath. She had the night mapped out for us already. I guess she was making plans long before I even arrived, I assumed with a slight hard on. That's what Miranda did to me every minute, every hour, and every second I was around her. – She made me horny.

She put a finger to her lips, for me to shut up.

"My father is on the phone, stupid," she whispered, slowly easing her perfect little coke bottle frame into the Jacuzzi. As she entered the warm water, she grimaced at the sting. The desire to seduce me was all in her eyes.

"Vonny!" Capo Dona screamed in the phone. I caught a glimpse of her titties floating like balloons on top of the water.

"What's up?" I asked, staring eye to eye with his beautiful daughter who was inches in front of me.

Knowing her dad was on the phone, I was trying hard to relax. However, Miranda's juicy breast had nipples that were a dark brown, and rested against her almond tone tanned skin. They were erect and pointy, and the moment felt very uncomfortable for me.

"Son, I'm in the jet!" he replied through a static filled call. *Man, why did he have to call me son*? I wondered, thinking about how Miranda had just stepped out of the Jacuzzi butt-ass naked. She was standing directly in front of me, looking fine as ever. When she walked away, I watched as her pretty feet left small wet prints on the marble stone. Then as Capo Dona continued, I was quickly brought back to reality. "Vonny, it's been a sudden change of plans!" The line became quiet for a moment. Then he continued. "Hello… are you still there?" he asked.

"Yeah Boss. I'm listening, - Un'hu, I'm still here," I assured him as my eyes shifted towards his daughter, who was over at the mini-bar. I nodded at Miranda, and sipped on a glass of red wine that she'd just brought over from the bar. I have to admit, Miranda impressed me. After seeing her with no clothes on, I was able to really see what she had going on. And man was she gorgeous. Hell, a stallion even, or better yet, maybe even a pretty little dime-piece all in one package. I gave her a smile, while I continued to talk with her dad. I mean, in the back of my mind, I always held that promise to Capo Dona that I'd never go into her. And because our relationship was solidified around trust and loyalty, being accepted as an apprentice under him was one thing I cherished more than anything.

"It's late there and I really don't like to be discussing business during non-working hours like this, Vonny. But the show must go on."

As Capo Dona began a dialogue for my detail, his lovely innocent daughter whom he loved and trusted so much was doing a raunchy, and far from innocent act with her feet underwater. She had her toes massaging and rubbing all between my legs. I just sipped wine and listened to my boss until he finished talking. Before I could speak again, Miranda had her toes, all over my scrotum. My sack rested on her toes like cherries on a stem. I was enjoying the small little erotic demonstration she did with my family jewels, which caused a moment of silence between the boss and I.

"Capo Dona !" I said, without waiting on his reply. "Can I drive one of your cars for a while?"

"Which one?"

"The Audi!"

"What's wrong with your car...? The Audi is new!"

"Boss, something came up," I muttered. "I just need to park it for a few days. Trust me. I'll tell you about it later." Miranda's eyes met mine. I didn't know if I'd said too much around her or not, but Capo Dona got straight to the point.

"Okay, take the Audi A8 and leave the Benz alone! I haven't driven any of them yet. And be careful out there, Vonny."

A smile crept on my face.

"Sure thing, Boss!" I replied, and then the line went dead.

After that last sexual encounter with Soul, I had to be extra careful when dealing with Miranda. Her young self was too hot for her own good. Since she was still a virgin, seeking for somebody to put out her flame, I held her at arm's length, because I valued my life more than anything; especially after dealing with her father who was the crime boss of the entire ninth circuit.

"Miranda stop!" I stood up out of the Jacuzzi with a ferocious hard on. Her eyes were fixed on what was dangling between my legs.

"Where are you going, it's after one in the morning?" she questioned, pulling at my wrist for me to stay. "Come here and let me touch it."

"Miranda I'm going home," I grumbled, drying myself off with her robe. Afterwards, I slipped on my gear that Dexter had neatly folded and draped across a lounge chair. I noticed there was a Nike sweat shirt lying next to my clothes, so I put that on too. Miranda looked disappointed, but I was looking out for everyone's well being; mine especially.

"I'm taking your dads' Audi and leaving my car here," I explained, handing her the key to my car. "Where are your father's keys?"

Her hair was all naturally kinky and was real curly once it got wet.

"He leaves them in the glove compartment." She turned her nose up at me.

Damn she looks so good, I thought to myself walking towards the garage port, then I paused and ducked behind an old grandfather clock to watch as she stepped her naked body out of the water. As she dried off, steam filled the room. Her nipples were as hard as small marbles, and very erotic to me. The site was so stimulating, a sinful rage of lust boiled deep within me. I wanted to go grab that pretty young thang and lusciously kiss her soft innocent lips, but I knew deep in my heart that that could never happen, not right now anyways. Surely if anybody found out about us, the outcome would be horrific. I had to keep things professional at all times.

When I sat behind the brand new Audi A8, I felt like I was in a totally different world. When it came to a car, I was not use to all the technical stuff that made it seem like I was in the cockpit of an airplane. And as I sat behind the wheel, I never felt a bump on the road. The ride was extremely smooth, and before long, I'd made it home. I was excited to be driving in a $85,000 dollar vehicle. I was so excited that I even had the nerve to park my luxurious sports car in one of my neighbors stall.

Damn! Vonny, you got some nerve, I thought, smiling as I entered my front door.

CHAPTER 10

Saturday, December 4th

After my apprenticeship, I'm supposed to be considered as a professional for the Black Illuminati. Killing would soon become my new trade. As I drove I-15 East to Las Vegas, the next morning, I had a lot of things scrambling through my mind.

"Here you want to hit this?" I struggled to say. He stared at the blunt, then at me, and then at the blunt again.

When I passed the blunt full of chronic to Lefty Bull, there was smoke filled deep within my lungs.

"Man I thought you were on parole?" he responded, grabbing the blunt to take a long drag, and then handed it back to me.

"Don't trip. My parole agent is off for the holidays. And thanks for coming out to Vegas with me."

It was silent for a moment, and then Lefty seemed like he was already high after only one hit.

"Man, get up!" I yelled, rolling down the windows so the air could stimulate him. Lefty didn't move or nothing. *Some people just can't smoke that good weed*, I thought to myself, as we cruised down the dark highway, playing a song by Amanda Perez.

***

The night was real dark and quiet, which gave me a little time to think about what was going on. I had to figure out a safe way to make sure this rub off was successful. First, I had to be able to maintain a high degree of secrecy, and the good thing about my job was that I could come in from out of town, knock off a victim, disappear without a trace, and leave authorities without a suspect, which would make prosecuting someone out of the question.

Unfortunately, my federal drug conviction not only put me in a position to struggle and never be legit again, but also forced me to stay on my P's & Q's out here. Never would I be on the right side of the law again. In fact, the whole judicial system was a disgrace; that is from your local police force, to the money hungry lawyers all the way down to the scandalous secret society of elite judges. Their purpose is to give people extended fines and prison sentences, knowing that what they're doing is unconstitutional. And that's my description of the law.

It is what it is; so I am what I am. No more home invading or flockin'. The Black Illuminati has now become my new religion', I smiled, taking out a Camel cigarette and lit it. Suddenly, from the rear view mirror, blue and red lights were flashing. They were heading in our direction, and at top speed. From habit, I happened to glance at the speedometer to see how fast we were going.

"Damn it Lefty, get up! One-Time!" I nervously screamed, shaking his shoulder.

"The main thang is not to panic," he said, springing up from his sleep. "Damn, I brought two birds of that raw in my suitcase."

"You what!" I yelled out in disbelief, since I wasn't in my car.

To hear him speak those words drained all hope right out of me. This just couldn't be happening right now, I thought, resenting the thought of pulling the car over. From the rear view mirror, a Highway Patrol vehicle was trailing so closely behind us that the front bumper hit the back of our car, forcing me to pull over.

"5...4...3...2...1," I counted, cautiously pulling the Audi over to the right edge of I-15. From past experiences, I knew trying to run from One-Time in the hot desert was a no go. All I could think about at the time was jail and federal prison all over again. When the car came to a complete stop, I immediately put my hands on the steering wheel, looking brazen as ever. Lefty sat up in his seat as straight as he could, and put on his seatbelt. I guess for the officers, two black men driving around in a brand new Audi A8 sports car just didn't register correctly. Of course, this is a stolen car stop, or maybe even a car-jacking stop. I'm figuring that's what the officers were thinking when they pulled us over.

Since I had the Tec-9 at my house, Lefty was packing either his .25 automatic or a Glock.

"Kick back, I got my license," I told him before an early morning shootout occurred between us and the law boys.

Before taking this trip to Vegas, I'd gone on a shopping spree. I mean, I wanted to fuck off some money, so I copped myself a very rare white-gold Panerai Luminor watch piece. Only two of its kind in the world, and a nice Mondera blood diamond pinky ring. The only reason I bought the ring was because of the brotherhood. I was trying to imitate the crime bosses. My iced out jewelry cost way too much. The watch I bought took me for $14,000 and the ring got me for $2,000, with a deal, and because I had cash on hand, I paid $15,000.

Approaching our vehicle from the rear was a tall dark-skinned cop, wearing a light yellowish-brown State of Nevada Highway Patrol uniform. He also had out a .357 revolver, as he slowly crept up on my side of the car. *Damn, that's all we need is a black nervous cop,* I thought to myself. Those are always the ones who'll show off for the white guys.

Everything Is Everything by Lauryn Hill was bumping through the state of the art Bio-Sound speakers, so as he approached the car, I turned down the music. This was real, so I thought this was going to be how I went out.

"Driver! With your left hand, turn off the ignition!" The house niggah yelled instructions directly to me. I sighed, let out a deep breath of frustration, and followed instructions. I looked over and saw Lefty with his right hand on the butt of his gun.

"Now driver, slowly step out of the vehicle!" he screamed, staring at my every move. Observing the way he spoke into his walkie talkie, I knew more officers were on the way. "Get your face down up against the car!" he said. As I leaned over on the side of the car, he handcuffed me and threw me into the backseat of his patrol car.

Seconds later, another Highway Patrol vehicle pulled up. The high beams were on extra bright, lighting up the entire backseat of the car. I also noticed it was a K-9 Unit, because I could hear vicious barking going on. Quickly I had to come up with a plan to get us out of this mess. Capo Dona was going to be pissed off at me; especially if he found out that his new car was confiscated for a drug related arrest. I had on my side one of the cell-phone guns, so I figured I still was in good shape. As I watched them pull Lefty Bull out of the Audi by his shirt collar, two cops began beating the crap out of the homey with Billy clubs. Blood splatter flew everywhere. They beat him down so much that a puddle of blood accumulated on the warm pavement. He laid on the ground soaked in blood and unconscious. His eyes were closed, and from where I was seated, I noticed that one of his teeth appeared to be missing. Actually, it was lying right next to the side of his face on the ground.

With Lefty out, the officers approached the car I was in. I figured I was next to experience their torture. A frail mulatto, half breed officer, wearing eye glasses opened my door.

"Get out!" he roared, yanking on my arm. It felt as if he was trying to rip my arms off. The handcuffs were already on way too tight, so I knew they were up to no good.

"Say Joe, that one has a nice watch on." The dark skinned cop said.

While both cops stood there wondering what to do next with us, I thought of a plan lightning quick.

"It's yours if you let us go," I suggested. "Man, we'll forget about everything if you just let us both walk." I suggested, looking over at Lefty on the ground. It looked as if he was barely breathing, so I wanted to try to get him some help. "Let us walk away, I won't remember anyone's name or nothing!" I begged, pleading for our freedom.

If it's one thing I hate doing in this world is begging another man for something; especially a cop. Standing on the right side of me the officer held a large Ziploc bag with two kilo's of raw powder cocaine in it. Everyone went silent; especially me once he stuck his finger in the bag and brought it back to his tongue for a taste.

"Boy, that watch better be worth something, because this here is a whole lot'a dope," Officer Bookman indicated, flashing a hideous grin.

"I spent fourteen-grand for it!"

The dark-skinned cop who did most of the assault on Lefty Bull pulled out a cigarette and lit it.

"The great state of Nevada is a private family run institution. And we don't like you California boys coming in from out of town.

dealing your dope out here." He stomped out half a cigarette in the dirt. "We are private!" he yelled directly in my face, so that his nose grazed mine. I got a whiff of alcohol and foul cigarette smoke on his breath, and knew they didn't have to tell me twice. I picked it up the first time and read between the lines, which meant it was highly likely that they indulged in only a legal underground economy that thrived under a mass of complex rules of gambling. People come to Las Vegas to gamble and spend all their life's fortune on an easy come up.

"Here take the watch!" I demanded, "And leave me and my friend alone."

As I attempted to unfasten the Panerai watch from my wrist, the mulatto officer bitch slapped me as hard as he could across the face. Then he unlocked the handcuffs, and slid them off, along with my diamond ring. Since my complexion wasn't that dark, I had a pinkish-red hand print across the side of my face. I felt like taking off on the clown, but declined instead feeling satisfied that we were not going to jail. So like a real soldier, I took one for the team, because that's what we do.

Each officer jumped in his own patrol car and rapidly sped off, causing gravel and dirt to pop all over us. The lights were off in the Audi, so I couldn't see how bad the inside looked.

"Come on Lefty, this ground is hot. Let's get out of here," I softly uttered, pulling my homeboy off the ground.

He had blood all on the front side of his clothes, in his hair, and on his face. There was no way to describe Lefty's condition, other than, fucked up. On the front passenger's seat they left us one kilo of dope, which was the one that the mulatto opened up to taste. I grabbed the Ziploc bag and threw it on the floor next to an ice cooler we'd brought along with us.

"Damn, we took a loss. The bag is short," I said, and then added, "Homie, I'm into adding, not this subtracting shit!"

"Did they get most of it?" Lefty asked, leaning his head on me.

"Naw, just one brick." I assured him, lifting one of his legs to help him slide into his seat. The movement was all in one smooth motion. I shot a quick glance at Lefty's face and instantly felt sorry for him.

"Hand me a brew?" I asked, reaching in the back seat for a towel to wipe the blood from his face. His eye looked like a golf ball was under the skin, he looked really bad.

"Man here, hold your face with this, and get some ice out of the cooler to put over that eye!"

He nodded and grabbed for the towel.

After cleaning up and arranging things back in order, I got behind the wheel and started the motor. The incident that had just occurred only confirmed that the dope game was a game I needed to stay away from. The drug trade was bad for business, and the shit was no good and a very degrading investment.

"Next time, we gotta be more careful," I told my childhood friend, opening up the motor to speeds well past 100 MPH. "Hold on..."

CHAPTER 11

We cruised off of superhighway I-15, making it into the Las Vegas metropolitan downtown area at seven o'clock in the morning. To me this large oasis of land was only here to serve one countless purpose. To get rid of the rat Mobie "Dique" Lewis. And that was it! I came out here on strict conglomerate orders from the commission. Don business, not pleasure. Mobie had to go. Coincidentally, it was too bad for him that my reputation depended on his survival; besides, my newly entered apprenticeship was at stake here.

As we drove down Fremont Blvd. all the pimps, pushers, drug addicts and prostitutes stared at our car with curiosity as to who we were. It was clear that this was their turf and they were ready to defend it. Since the fight was taking place over at the new Mandalay Bay, my plan was to station Lefty Bull here. The old strip was out of the way, and I could put him in one of the old hotels, which would be our headquarters while in Vegas. Anyways, after that beat down, he needed to get some rest and regain his composure.

While I went to handle my business, Fremont Plaza was the perfect spot for him to do that. The old hotel sat directly at the top of the block. It was out of the way and low-key enough for a traveler just needing to gamble a little, or for someone in need of some local exotic call girls, free liquor, you know that sort of thing, I glanced over at Lefty.

"Man, I don't know how we did it, but we made it," I said pulling up to the hotel's glamorous entrance.

Mysteriously, out of nowhere a red-headed bellboy approached the car.

"This is valet parking, Sir," he said looking in the vehicle at Lefty's monstrous appearance and quickly backing up.

"Don't worry, we're staying," I stated, sarcastically, but very serious. We got out, got our key and headed to the elevator. "You can rest up in the room." I suggested, helping the homey out of the seat. His equilibrium was still off balance.

"Hold up. Hold up!" Lefty, loudly moaned. "I have a headache, so take it slow," he fussed.

I tipped the bellboy a healthy $50.00 bill, then he helped me with Lefty.

"Give me a second!" I told them both, heading back to the car to go in the trunk to get the kilo of dope out.

While there I stumbled across a peculiar army green backpack that I'd never seen before. It was under the spare tire, so I grabbed that too. It was awfully heavy, so I wondered why the police didn't find it. Back at the front counter, Lefty accompanied by our hired help was asking a sexy blonde employee questions about our room arrangements. When I heard him tell her that he wanted one on the top floor, I butted in.

"Excuse me Miss. But he's with me. We would like to acquire your Presidential Suite," I replied, sounding sophisticated with proper English.

"Okay, do you need something else?" She turned to look at me and waited for me to respond.

"Yes, will we be overlooking the east or west end of the city?" I questioned, sounding debonair and businesswise, which was a little somethin' somethin' that I picked up from Dexter.

The petite, slim receptionist had a very beautiful smile, which showed her perfectly straight, beautiful white teeth. Her attitude was cheerful and her warm, sensitive, deep sapphire blue eyes had me.

"We have two Presidential Suites I see, Mr ...?" She paused, and her head was down. As she stared at the computer, she nodded her head as if she was waiting for me to pronounce my last name.

"Plot!" I replied.

She wrote down something, and then repeated my name, "Plot."

"P.L.O.T." I spelled. "With just one T."

She looked up from the computer. "Okay Mr. Plot, we do show that your suite is available. This is an old hotel, so unfortunately, we only have two," she smiled, glancing back down at the computer screen. "And the suite you're in is located on our South West wing, which entirely overlooks Fremont Blvd."

"Sounds great!" I immediately replied, ready to get up to the room. She looked up one more time.

"So, how many nights are you here?"

"We'll just have to play that by ear, Sweetheart."

She flashed that beautiful smile, and then printed me a receipt with $1,026.15 shown as my deposit. I liked her spunk, but then she rudely yawned almost as if she was bored with me, or like I was possibly wasting her time. Her eyes surveyed me counting out my money.

"Have a nice stay here at Fremont Plaza," she said, picking up the front desk line after a short ring. Lucky for her the homey was in bad shape.

"Come on, Lefty. We don't got too far to go."

He leaned up against me for support. I excused the bellboy, so that he could get back to work. As we both stepped onto the elevator to head up to our suite, a couple of our old school friends, Swamp Bugg and Larry Luv stepped in with us.

"What floor?" Larry Luv asked, standing next to the floor keypad. From a glimpse, I noticed that they both were sweating, they seemed nervous about something, which made me uncomfortable.

"Top floor," I casually stated.

"Man, we saw those police beating y'all up earlier on the freeway," Bugg said grinning. I looked at him like he was crazy. "Man, that was ya'll, right?"

Lefty, holding his rib cage, struggled to speak.

"Why ya'll didn't stop then?"

"Because the Yukon we was in was dirty," Larry Luv added.

"Come to think of it, when One-Time had me in the back of the other patrol car, I did notice an all White Yukon 4X4 driving by real slow, almost to a creep.

"Whose is this?" Bugg was holding up my iced out Panerai sports watch in his hand. I was surprised as hell. "Man, don't ask no questions, but we sacked both they asses cause we caught'um slipping!" he coldly expressed.

"Good looking out, y'all get the ring," I smiled, sliding my watch back on.

"Don't trip, just stay out of trouble out here in Vegas." Larry Luv insisted, not responding to my other question.

I nodded and so did Lefty Bull. Bugg pushed the button for the elevator to stop on the seventh floor. When it did, I watched as they both stepped out. Upon exiting, neither said a word to us, or to each other.

   Finally, we made it up to the very top floor, and stepped out real slow. When the elevator's double doors closed, we noticed how the atmosphere all of a sudden took a drastic change from ordinary to extravagant. I never knew you encountered all this luxury, on the top floors of hotels. Shoot, way up here, a person couldn't help but notice the caliber of high quality living the rich experienced.

   On the wall, directly in front of the elevator was two arrows. One pointed to the West Wing and the other to the East. The carpet was so clean that it appeared to have never been walked on before. There was a bright summer peach color, and lining the carpet was exclusive Italian limestone that made a path leading into each of the suites. Over to the side was a cozy sitting area with a glass coffee table that was surrounded by soft peach couches for lounging. It was so peaceful that I felt a little out of place.

   We followed the limestone into a spacious ultra luxurious suite. Once inside, the floor transformed into a highly polished hard marble. The suite was equipped with a balcony that overlooked the entire west side of Las Vegas' metropolitan casino and gambling area. This place was like a private retreat. Again, I could not get over how peaceful it was this high up.

   The living room featured state of the art furniture and accessories, with a 72" Plasma flat screen that had surround sound, an Aiwa DVD/CD system, a Dell computer with high speed internet access, and a fireplace that sat directly in the middle of our two bedrooms. Mine had four London Fog raincoats and four Wilson leather coats hanging in the closet; there was also a pint of Dolce & Gabbana cologne sitting on the marble bathroom counter. After taking a long piss, I threw myself on the soft king size to relax for awhile.

   Back in the old days, Fremont Blvd. was the Mecca for your average pimp, player, and prostitute to enjoy their stay while in the Sin City area. That was way before the ethnic minority succession took place. Some people call the Black and Mexican gangs the new Mafias. Each year, street gang's assets total profit was in the millions. So these menace to society guys were respected as urban ghetto superheroes. They are glorified in other countries, in Hip Hop music, R & B music, and amongst their peers who still reside back in their old neighborhoods. Lately, for some odd reason, tabloids have been glamorizing their thuggish tattoos, their drug money, and their illegal dealer status as major criminals of today.

If only the old mobster, Bugsy Siegel could see Vegas right now. I bet had the I.R.S. or greedy F.B.I. not been breathing down his neck, the old timer would've been real proud of himself today, I thought, looking over the balcony to breathe in the hot desert air. I noticed people down below scrambling around like tiny ants, and smiled because everything seemed better from the top.

While I checked to see what was in the green backpack, Lefty attended to his face in the bathroom. Once I discovered there was a lot of cash banded together, I was in shock. There was over $200,000 that I was responsible for. With that in mind, I headed over to a mini-bar, before I decided to make a phone call.

"Are you alright in there?" I yelled through the door, checking on Lefty. There was no answer. I believe his ego was bruised. "Lefty, are you Okay?" I yelled a second time, grabbing the ice bucket to go to the machine. "I'm going down the hall to go get some ice!" I said, but still I got no response at first.

"Don't forget your key!" he shouted, over the sound of running water.

"Okay, I'm out," I said, closing the door behind myself.

As I walked down the long corridor, for some odd reason Miranda popped into my mind? Unexpectedly, I felt a slight warmth inside. It was probably from the stiff shot of Vodka I'd just downed.

My thoughts shifted back to the money. Dang, real friends are hard to find nowadays, especially intelligent ones. That's a whole bunch of cash money I left back in the suite with him, but if I can't trust Lefty, then I can't trust nobody. Besides, as long as we are both out here alone, right now, we're all we got.

The ice machine was next to a lounge that had an old fashioned telephone booth. It was a phone booth that they had installed when the place was built. It was an antique for real. It had the old roller dial with the separate mouth piece. I was really fascinated with the booth, it was empty, so I stepped in and sat down. It had a wet mildew smell to it, so before making the call, I lit a Camel cigarette.

"Hello…" Dexter answered, accepting the call.

"Dexter! This is Vonny."

"Mr. West, glad to hear from you," he politely replied.

"Have you heard anything from the boss?" I asked, pleased that I'd gotten through so fast.

"Yes! Vonny, Master Dona has instructed me to forward your call to him ASAP." Dexter put me on hold, and then the two of us patiently waited for him to pick up. "He's on the plane, so it may take a minute."

After about the tenth ring, somebody finally picked up.

"D & C Reality," the person answered. Surprisingly, a female's voice that I'd never heard before was on the other line. Her voice was soft and sweet. Dexter was to the point.

"Madam Constance is Capo Dona available?" he asked.

That's why I felt so comfortable around Dexter. He was a polished butler who always stayed in his place. His knowledge of what was going on alone, and his ability to keep things discrete was a testament to his loyalty to the conglomerate. Suddenly, static interrupted our call.

"Hold on please!" she put us on hold.

It was silent for a brief minute, then someone got on the phone, shattering glasses and muffled voices could be heard in the background.

"He said that he's in a very important business meeting with a few new partners, so he wanted me to take all messages." Constance charmingly stated. "Can I take your name and number. Capo Dona will get back to you shortly?"

"This is Vonny!" I informed her, glancing around the lounge.

"Oh… so you're the Vonny West that everybody's been talking about. Glad to meet you. Your boss has been waiting for you to call, hold on-for a second." *Damn, she sounds attractive over the phone*, I thought. "Oh yeah, by the way this is Constance Lynn!" she added, as if I was pressed for conversation.

"Ask Capo Dona what should I do with the green backpack?"

"Hold on, please." Constance said.

Besides the low muffled chitchat in the background, it sounded like a formal banquet was taking place on the plane. The smooth sounds of Jazz leisurely added to the call.

"Have you ever seen Constance before, Dexter?" I asked, putting out the cigarette.

"No I have not," he quickly replied. "But I'm sure she's a beauty."

"Dexter, I wonder what Capo Dona has to say?" I added, feeling a little jumpy.

"Young Lad, just be patient. Besides, patience is what so many others respect about us."

Finally, our conversation was interrupted by a male's voice.

"Vonny!" Capo Dona responded excited to hear from me.

I laughed and was happy to hear my boss' voice.

"Dexter is on three-way."

"Hey Dex...! What's up at home?" he asked, with so much positive energy. It was almost as if he didn't have a care in the world.

"Everything is everything, Sir." Dexter responded. "The ship is sailing on its usual course. Moving full steam ahead, I might add."

"Perfect! Now that's a beautiful thing. Let everybody at home know that I'm doing fine and that I send my love. Also, tell my daughter that I haven't forgotten about her. And that I'm bringing her back a souvenir from Canada."

"Sure will, Sir." Dexter softly replied over a bunch of static.

The moment was silent for a few seconds, which was due to a wave of static.

"Vonny!...Vonny! Are you still there?" the boss yelled.

"I'm here Boss. I'm right here," I answered.

"About that bag, Vonny." He was sincere and to the point. "Don't ask me any questions about where it came from. You just be extremely careful, and make sure you take care of yourself out there. Son, this is a reality. Everything that is going on around you right now is real."

"I know it's real," I quickly stated.

"Let me talk. I don't know how long this line will stay connected!" he griped, eager to get down to business.

"Okay Boss, what's up?"

"Needless to say, in this part of your life, you have incidentally inherited a great deal of difficulty. For men change, hoping to better ourselves, but we also hope that we are not deceived. You know that because of our actions, sometimes by experience we find that we can go from bad to worse." As Capo Dona spoke, I slipped off into deep thought. He's telling me the truth, because once I put a gun in my hand I killed with it, and I didn't even expect too either. The situation just happened that way. "You, like a few other crime bosses have been in prison before and are fortunate enough to get one more shot at life. Vonny, a lot of people are not that fortunate.

There are only two types of people that are ever released from prison, the broken men and those who have done their very best to maintain themselves. No one who leaves prison is ever normal again. And never could you be the same person you were before you were incarcerated. Of course you already are quite aware of the fact that you are a part of an elite group of men. A system that is a real team. We are a secret society of underground assassins. Our way of life is murder for hire, and we operate on orders that are top secret---"

A little static disturbed our call again. I stared at the bucket in my hand, but did not say a word. Finally he continued. "After you do this job, you must fall back and exclude yourself from your old lifestyle. All of your old relations, and most importantly, your old thuggish acquaintances must cease." Capo Dona spoke as clear as he could. "You do understand the reasons behind me telling you all this, don't you Vonny?"

"He understands clearly, Sir," Dexter quickly butted in.

Now we we're talking! I thought to myself.

"So that's why you put me up under the familial?" I questioned, feeling a positive vibe from our conversation.

"I told you the history before about your natural father leading our conglomerate in the 70's. Right! Well, now let's get down to the bag issue. You know we all move large quantities of money. Vonny West as soon as you advance more into your apprenticeship, develop a gifted craft, then you also will be on board moving large amounts of cash along with the rest of us. We have accounts in different parts of the country and abroad. Because of the secrecy act in Switzerland, I'm going to tell you that that is where our main banking is done. The older Don's and I are always looking for new investors. We have very wealthy people who rely heavily on us for financial backing. They invest and depend on our leadership. I'm speaking of the silent money. That illegal green bag has to be hidden under radar. We deal with local politicians, senators, Supreme Court judges, doctors, lawyers, and the list goes on. You got it?"

"Yeah, I got it!" I quickly said.

"That sack of money you found in the car was a policy write off from another profitable business expenditure I'm involved in. After speaking with a few of the Don's, we came to a conclusion regarding giving you a chance."

"A chance?" I asked, more as a statement.

"Just invest the money wisely," he stated in a fatherly fashion. "That was part of our plan for you, Son," he informed me, as the line started dying out between us again.

"Tele-waves do that a lot, when you're crossing over into other countries and different time zones." Dexter explained.

"Would it be a wise decision to buy land here in Vegas?" I asked, trying to get more advice on what it was that they wanted me to do with their money.

The line was silent for a moment.

"Don't forget that we are a team." Capo Dona emphasized. "I figure that you can find a commercial building that we can set up, renovate to your taste, and design it to be a place that you'll have plenty of space to use for your Wall Street trading."

"For me." I smiled at the thought of the family giving me financial backing to run and manage my very own investment firm. I had to go find a building quick, and set up shop before they changed their minds. Capo Dona sensed the excitement in my voice.

"Son, trust all my wisdom and better judgment. But use your own wisdom and follow the paths that the familial has paved for you already. An apprentice ought to have no other goal than to follow instructions, perfect his craft, and become favored among the class of great leaders in the history of Dons."

"I clearly understand what you're getting at, Boss," I grinned. 'It's time for me to grow up."

"And remember to never go past the mark you aim for. In this business, never be greedy. Set a goal, and when you get there stop!" he explained.

"I got it, Boss."

"I couldn't have said it better myself!" Dexter added. The line went quiet for a few seconds.

"Is that all, Boss?" I respectfully inquired.

"That's it." Capo Dona's voice went flat. "You're on federal parole, so the feds will be watching your every move. Remember Vonny, whatever you do from now on will reflect on us. Understand?"

"I understand, Boss. Don't worry. I got this!" I exclaimed, ready to get off the phone. It was time to take care of business and grow my leaf on the family tree. You know, set my mark, because this was my time to make it to the top of the success ladder.

A few seconds later, the line went dead. Dexter and I were the only two on the line again.

"Does your room have Internet access?" he softly asked.

"Yeah."

"Well, for future reference, Mister West that's how we will chat from now on. So whenever you're on assignment, use that. Deal?"

"Deal!" I said, and then hung up.

I got the ice, and headed back to the room. Once I got there, Lefty had opened up a fifth of Seagram's Gin and was filling up an empty beacon.

"I see you're feeling better, here's some ice cubes."

"Man, look at my face!" he belligerently yelled, turning around for me to get a good look at him. "I can't go out looking like the Elephant Man." Out of anger, a tear rolled down the side of his face.

As I looked at him, I wondered if his face stung from his tears, because the whole right side of his face was bluish-purple, and his upper lip was bruised and the size of a bolder marble. There was little he could do to stop the bleeding from his nose, but his lip needed sutures. "Do you want me to call a doctor?" I asked, feeling sorry for him. I had to admit, I was stunned at his monstrous appearance.

"No! Man, I don't want you to call anyone!" he screeched. "Say Vonny, do you think that Bugg or Larry Luv got away with that dope One-Time took from us?"

I couldn't believe what I'd just heard.

"Man chalk that up as a loss!" I fussed, as his eyes met mine.

"Whatever man."

I picked up the telephone and pushed 0.

Without warning, Lefty built up enough strength to snatch the receiver from my hand. At six-feet, he had a horrifying appearance, and looked like something out of a late night horror flick, so because of that I refused to argue or struggle with him for the phone. That was his face not mine.

"I still feel that you at least need some stitches!" I told his ornery ass.

"Don't worry. All I need is to let the swelling go down a little."

I ignored him. Lefty's a grown man. If he wants to act stubborn and act like a big baby, then that's on him. And anyways, before it got too late, I had to count up the money in the green backpack.

"Pour me a shot of whatever it is that you're drinking," I requested, casually walking towards my sleeping quarters.

"How you want it?"

"Straight up!"

Everything seemed perfect, like I was in my very own safe haven. All of the lavish living I was doing was deinstitutionalizing me; from the air conditioned suite, the marvelous marble bathroom, to the large DVD plasma screen. *For Real*, I thought, as stacks and stacks of cash money came tumbling out of the backpack. Everything from $100 big faces to two-dollar bills was on the bed, just waiting to get counted. With the fight starting in just four hours, I needed Lefty to help me count up all the dough, and we needed to move fast doing it.

Lefty stood motionless at the doorway, holding both drinks in his hands.

"Man, I have to go take care of some business, so we need to hurry up and count this up." I mentioned, gripping a knot of $1's and $5's in my hand. "This is what we're gon gamble with!" I said, throwing a stack to the side.

"No problem homeboy. Let's get to work," Lefty downed his shot of Gin in one swallow.

I eased the sack closer to me thinking about how I loved my childhood crew, and that it was too bad that after this trip, I'd have to move on and separate myself, based on the instructions I'd gotten earlier.

CHAPTER 12

It took us two long hours to count, sort, and band up several $20,000 bundles of cash. When we were done, we came up with a total of $291,000 in cash. I put $290,000 in the backpack, and then a thousand dollar on the shelf near the computer. Glancing at my watch, I couldn't help but notice it was exactly one hour until show time. Since I felt uncomfortable about leaving Lefty alone, without his knowledge, I called an escort service for him.

"Are you sure you're going to be okay in here by yourself?" I asked, dialing the number.

"Yeah, don't trip. It's a lot to do around here," Lefty said, disappointed that he couldn't go with me to the fight.

"Don't open the door for nobody!" I replied, clowning around with him.

By this time, I'd changed, and was standing in a large three picture mirror, adjusting the collar on my new Valentino shirt. I finished getting dressed extremely slow, because of the special surprise I'd lined up for my boy. Plus, when she walked in, I wanted to be here to see the expression on his face.

"Okay Uncle Vonny!" he teased.

"It should be a good fight, what'cha think?" I muttered, rushing to put on my shoes.

"It should be."

Finally, there was a knock at the door. She tapped seven times, which was the code I'd told the company to use.

"Lefty get the door!" Based on what had happened earlier, the homey grabbed his Glock pistol, making sure to answer the door with it in his possession.

"Relax!" I told him. "It's a surprise for you."

"How you know?"

"Because, I gave her a code and told her to knock seven times."

"Damn! Vonny, I'm not in no shape to be seeing somebody right now." He backed away from the door, and rushed to his room to hide himself.

"To hell with you!" I replied, after peeping through the tiny hole to confirm that it was her. Slowly, I unlocked the door. That was something that I'd picked up from Dexter. He always told me that whenever you have an unfamiliar guest come to your home, never rush to let them in. Instead, you let them ease their selves in; that way they never know what to expect.

I stood at the mini-bar in the far corner of the room, to give it one more inspection.

"Come in!" I invited her in, pouring us both drinks. Just like Dexter said, she crept in real slow. "Glad that you could make it," I greeted her with my voice soft, sounding genuine and debonair at the same time.

She turned in the direction of my voice off of impulse. This woman was drop dead gorgeous. She was sexy, very grown, had nice breast that sat high on her, with skin the color of silky smooth coco. She was wearing open toe sandals that exposed a gold toe ring, which I found very sexy. The evening gown she wore was sophisticated. It fit tight and elegant, hugging every curve of her body. Her eyes surveyed the place to quickly determine what was going on.

I walked from the dimly lit corner, holding two glasses of Gin & Pineapple juice in hand.

"Don't be afraid. You can have a seat," I said, handing her a nearly empty glass. That was another thing Dexter taught me. When engaging a lady for cocktails, never pour her too much alcohol. According to him, that's tacky, and it's always important to be a gentleman first. He taught me to be mindful of the fact that first impressions meant a lot to a woman.

"Thank you," she said. "Are we going someplace formal, because they didn't tell me, if we are?"

"No… No…. No..." I stopped her. "I'm going out tonight. You and my cousin will be here alone." She glanced around, looking for another person. "Relax and make yourself comfortable," I suggested, almost forgetting my manners. "I'm so sorry beautiful. Please excuse my poor manners, but what is your name?"

She laughed.

"Doll!" she said, smiling as she took a sip of her drink. Trying to keep myself focused, I couldn't help but notice her remarkable green eyes, and her see through green gown which matched her eyes. I treated her like a special lady, as I reached for her soft hand. She obliged, and I respectfully kissed her delicate skin.

"My name is Vonny." My voice was gentle. "My cousin is in his living quarters right now. He's licking his wounds, and he's in pretty bad shape."

Her eyes gestured in the direction of the closed bedroom door.

"Meaning?" Doll was inquisitive of her reason for being here.

"Doll, he's hurt right now," I said, giving her minimal details, because the less she knew, the better off she was.

"I see," Doll crossed one leg over the other, exposing a thick thigh. "So I take it you want me to keep him company while you go out to play?" she asked, taking another tiny sip of Gin. "Sort'a like a nanny," she flirtatiously smiled at me with those pretty teeth of hers.

Before she made me do something out of character, I turned away.

"He's the lucky one. Hell, I'd stay hurt forever, just to have a nanny as gorgeous as yourself," I flirted, tightening up my two piece Armani suit. "How do I look?" I asked, turning from the mirror to show off my matching shoes and suspenders. Doll swallowed the last drop of liquor in her glass.

"You look handsome."

I walked back over to the counter I'd earlier put the $1,000 on, counted out five-hundred dollar bills, and then headed for the door, feeling a hint of jealousy towards Lefty. I'm only human. *Doll is fine!* I thought to myself. *Umm those wide hips, that soft ass, and her legs seem so smooth,* I fantasized while on the elevator. She was flawless in my eye sight, a flirtatious dime-piece, but the type of female who didn't even realize how fine and sexy she was. Doll was classy, and I recognized her style the moment we made eye contact and I could've stared into those green eyes and her cute freckles forever.

I hoped Doll is still there when I get back to the suite, I thought, listening to a jam by Chris Brown over the overhead intercom.

". . . all night!" I sang along, sitting in the lobby to patiently wait for the bellboy to bring me my ride.

On my way to the fight the hawk swept in. It cooled down to about 56-degrees, so it was kind of chilly outside. While driving, it was time to unwind and clearly think things out. Though so many people are in prison as a result of someone telling on them, for some strange reason, I didn't have a problem with doing this hit. Cats like him did the crime, but couldn't do the time, so like rats they cut deals to save self, and have no problem with making somebody else's life miserable, which is ridiculous to me. And the more I thought about it, I actually did want to sack that rat. Make him pay and peel his cap back.

Whenever I'm solo, I realized that a man could advance in life if he's willing to stay neat, clean shaven, and never tacky, which would prevent him from standing out like a sore thumb. With my new lifestyle came a new motto. My new motto was: always stay alone, even in public, if you're gonna live my type of lifestyle, do the things I do, and go places I like to go. My appearance is most important when I'm hired to do a job, I can never take an entourage with me, because they will attract too much attention, too much heat, and heat brings on problems that I don't need. I know some may view my life as reckless, exuberant even, but I live by the gun and try hard not to die by the gun. In staying incognito, I don't need nobody to have my back but my pistol. My gun is like a loyal big sister. Whenever I'm in trouble, she comforts me.

Enemies can get you killed, and a close friend can be like a parasite. They can get you wacked over night, so my trust is always in a person only to a certain extent.

In Las Vegas the Mandalay Bay Hotel & Resort is one of the most immaculate and highly glamorized boxing spots around. The time read 8:10 in the evening, so the preliminary matches had already started. The parking lot was full and it wasn't anywhere for me to park; even Valet Parking had a line of cars half a mile long, so I was forced to go down the block, park in a convenience store's lot, and then walk back. All of the entrance doors were jammed packed. It seemed as if everybody was trying to get in to watch Trinidad and Bell pound on each other. I managed to ease myself through the musty crowd and make it to the front of the line. I showed the security guard my front row V.I.P. pass, and then he let me by without any problems. I was so nervous as I neared the metal detector. I didn't know if I'd make it through without setting it off, due to the gun. *The last thing I needed is some negative attention tonight,* I nervously thought, placing the small weapon carefully on the contraband tray. After getting through the security screening process, I couldn't help but think to myself how easy that was. Smiling, I put my car key and gun back in my coat pocket. Before walking down to ring side I decided to casually stroll over to the restroom before getting comfortable.

Being that it was so crowded I figured that it was even more crowded down on the flats next to the boxing ring. From a glimpse I noticed that it was a lot of Latinos and Spanish speaking blacks in there that night. It looked like a little Tijuana, which made the line for the restroom seem endless. I hated crowds and being around a bunch of people, all up under me moving around so much. Suddenly, it was just my luck that eight or nine heads ahead of me in line was a guy who looked identical to Mobie "Dique" Lewis. He was accompanied by another tall well over six feet thuggish looking dude. I figured that dude to be Mobie's gunman, and since I only had four shots, I had to make every single bullet count.

Both guys were wearing black full length leather trench coats, talking loud, and making obnoxious jokes about each other. The two, Mobie especially, were acting as if they didn't have a care in the world. And the reason I knew it was Mobie up there was because of his hair. It was styled in cornrows going down both sides of his head which was the same way he wore his hair at Lompoc. People in society aren't too familiar with that prison look. One would only have to have been there before to know what I'm talking about.

For about five minutes, I waited in the cut over by a Pepsi machine relieved that nobody knew me. I couldn't believe how much of a coincidence it was to have my victim standing so close to me. Now all I needed to do was confirm that this was the right person, then its lights out for that snitch as soon as he stepped out of the restroom.

For some strange reason, visions of sitting in the Jacuzzi with Miranda clicked in my head. I had butterflies in my stomach from uncertain probabilities as if I wasn't ever going to see her ever again. She'd done something to me that night that words couldn't explain. Realizing how much she had my best interest at heart, I had it bad for her. Thinking of her made me miss her elegant style, and all that beauty, which was odd for such a person to keep my nose so wide open.

Suddenly, from out of nowhere, my victim barged out of the double doors of the restroom in a rage. Capo Dona had mentioned before that he liked to snort powdered cocaine, so after putting two-and-two together I figured that that could have a lot to do with his rambunctious behavior. *Things are going to get real ugly down here real soon*, I thought to myself, positioning my body where I'd meet his eyes squarely when he walked past me. I wanted him to be face to face before I shot him. He was only ten or fifteen feet away from me. My finger was itching so bad to pull the trigger that it itched deep inside.

It was silent for a moment. Everything seemed to have stopped. He stopped walking towards me to reach inside his coat pocket to pull out a small iPhone.

"Yeah!" he says, speaking loud and looking around so that everybody could notice him on the phone.

He was flamboyant, but also a snitch, so instead of moving up, he was going down. And it was my job to make sure that he looked up at the world from six-feet under the ground. I crept so close to Mobie talking on the phone that I could hear his complete conversation.

In reality a snitch ain't got no privacy. In prison a snitch ain't got no property. With that already understood, I had my victim mapped out completely. His lieutenant hadn't exited the restroom yet which left Mobie exposed. He was all alone for the taking.

Quickly, I made my move, whipping out the cell phone gun. I held it just inches from my victim's heart waiting for the perfect time to pull the trigger. Enough was enough. I'd made myself sick from looking at that buster.

Mobie glanced in my direction with a smirk on his face. He started opening a fresh pack of Camels, so I aimed and fired one .25 round into his jugular vein. The shot was quiet, then without delay he fell to his knees. He was still holding onto the iPhone, as he started to squirm with his eyes wide open.

"You snitch! You bitch motherfucka' you won't be telling on nobody no more will you." I knelt down next to the squirming body. Blood was pumping from the wound, "This is for all the real men that can't get to your scandalous ass." I spoke so only he heard me, before I shot him execution style two more times in the face.

The impact jerked his head back, locking his secrets in his brain forever. I stared down over the dead body for a brief moment of melancholy. This was an organized campaign thanks to me.

As I hovered over my first victim, Mobie's lieutenant came running towards me, so I waited and when he bowed lifeless, I fed one round in the middle of his forehead, killing him instantly. His body quickly collapsed on top of Mobie's dead body. *Pound for pound this is my new passion, my new way of life,* I thought staring down steadily at the two lifeless cadavers, both with their eyes still open. I had another silent moment of melancholy only this time this one was rushed.

A wave of nervousness started to shiver down my spine when all the guys started to gather around to look at the slaughter. Mayhem lingered in the air. There weren't any women around so that eliminated any sudden screaming and panicking that might have gone on.

Between us men it was just your average rub off hit professionally done because no visible artillery was ever seen. This was a high level job of success done by a low-key very casual killer. What's done was a done deal already, making everybody just mind their own business and keep the line moving to the restroom as if nothing was going on, which to me was a beautiful thing, so I casually slid off into the crowd to blend in. I was deeply pleased with myself that this job went as smooth as it did.

In the back of me as I was easily gaiting away there was a loud commotion that circled around the bodies.

"Get a doctor! They both need a doctor! One of 'um is still breathing!"

I never glanced back. Instead I quickly slipped through an emergency exit door, through an alley, walked down to the convenience store parking lot where my car was parked, and took a long exhausting piss by the Audi. I threw my ticket on the ground in front of me to get it soaked in urine.

At first my intentions were to drive off and rush back to the suite but declined. Instead I sat in the car and put on an old Dr. Dre 2001 CD, rolled up a fat chronic joint, and then lit it. As I sat taking pride in my work I smoked the spices all the way down to a roach. While watching the sideshow of cars in heavy traffic, I was comforted that nobody could see me, because the steel-blue Audi sat camouflaged in between a Maybach and a Jaguar. That's where I sat for hours until the fight was over with before driving off into the busy crowd of traffic.

Chapter 13

A friend of mine named Money who's a male stripper out here in Las Vegas told me about this club he dances at on ladies night called, *The Honeycomb*. He said that the top quality choice females of Vegas hung out there, and nothing but the best be in that place. He also, warned me to be suited and booted whenever I decided to go. As I cruised down the strip I happened to see the topless bar, so I quickly changed the course turning into some residential area to make sure that I wasn't being followed. In my line of work that came with the territory. One had to always play it safe. Health first everything else was second. After realizing that the coast was clear, I used the navigation system to guide me back towards the topless bar. Once there, I sat in the parking lot to watch the local news' broadcast about the double homicide on the TV before walking in.

The place was packed when I stepped in the joint. This was a rest haven full of glamorous women, they were upscale, and considered to be Sin City's finest. As I delightfully soaked up the moment, classy dime-pieces all had their eyes on me giving me so much undivided attention that my poise was off balanced a little; so very casually I stepped to one of the bar stools and quietly sat down next to a pimp partner I knew from out of the Bay area.

The pimp's name was Northcutt. He was from out of the San Francisco Bay area and was one of the most prosperous hustlers, with the finest set of girl's on this side of the West Coast. His bitches sold pussy all the way from the Bay to San Diego. He was even known to have Hollywood on lock. Since Northcutt was busy eying some new game, we spoke briefly, and I kept it moving towards the stage.

On the runway was a gorgeous young lady with seductive thick country thighs. A natural siren in her youth wearing raunchy cut up Daisy Dukes all up in her ass. She looked every bit of eighteen years old or maybe even younger. But that didn't stop the line of horny old men all lustfully desiring to see more of her climbing up and down the gold pole with her legs wide apart, she was nude throughout her whole pole routine, and of course she had a shaved coochie that all the perverts dreamed over. The horny old men threw $50 and $100 dollar bills on stage every which way, the young girl's legs seemed to pop open for them, which to me was disgusting because of how young the little blonde tramp was, and the fact that she was old enough to be their daughter or young grandchild was a disgrace.

But yet and still this is a strip club, a place to enjoy my special moment while I unwound and thought things over for awhile. I had to try relaxing my nerves, especially after looking at both my victim's eyes after they died. For me it was just another day at the office, I pondered reasonably, sipping on a glass of ice water, and watched as the youngster did her thang up there on stage. As my mind raced to start thinking about our elite secret outfit, and what a proper price for a murder contract was truly worth. A waitress came over to me. "Can I get you something to drink?" she politely asked, smelling good like fresh strawberries.

I turned slowly to her, nodded, then looked up into those green eyes and was stunned. "Doll!" I shouted over a loud Rihanna song. She followed me over to a small table.

"I just left Lefty at the room, maybe not even an hour ago," she said with a big smile on her face. "He wanted me to stay with him until you came back." I didn't blame him this girl was fine. "But I couldn't. I had to leave. As you can see Vonny, escorting is my day job. I work here in the club at night." Doll mentioned that with pride behind it. All her weight was leaning to one side with one free hand on her wide hip. She looked sassy and sexy at the same time, "so are you drinking or what?" she asked waiting for me to order.

"Yeah! I'll have your Gin on the rocks, with a side order of pineapple juice!" I explained being a little sarcastic. "You know what I drink!"

She went into business mode. While Doll started writing down my order on a small pad I noticed that she had a hickey bite on the right lower side of her neck. But she walked off before I went there. Besides of all the pretty ladies that were there that night Doll was still one of the prettiest females that I've ever seen in my entire life.

Up close and personal Doll's legs was one of her best features on her curvy body. I couldn't help but notice how her hips were shaped over her legs sashaying with a soft big butt that switched side-to-side when she walked away. Her legs looked smooth and soft, not like the other girl's who wore fish net stockings, Doll's legs were bare and muscled, and beautiful with no childhood scar marks on them. Just thinking of baby gave me a hard-on.

Suddenly, all the lights went out, making it pitch black, followed by neon-florescent red and pink stage lights flashing in every direction. Instantly every head turned towards the stage. A spot light was focused entirely on a sexy hot exotic dancer wearing sophisticated red-rimmed reading glasses. The song *Little Red Corvette* by the musician Prince came on over the loud speakers.

Stepping out from behind the evanescence of white smoke appeared to be a very attractive red-head with a big white ass, wearing a red garter belt, red fish net stockings, and red high heeled stiletto pumps that were soon kicked off as her routine climaxed. She was topless exposing creamy white ivory skin with voluptuous breasts that sat heavy. Her titties were so big that she could suck on them herself.

"Are you enjoying yourself, young man?" Doll came back sounding so sweet and precious. I noticed that her eyes had a sparkle. She put two glasses on the table and sat down. "Her name is Chance. She's from Amsterdam. Do you want me to introduce her to you?" she suggested, quite aware by now that I was enjoying Chance's dance routine. "She's single too!" Doll laughed.

I grinned.

"Nawh. I just dropped by the club because I needed time to myself. Besides Doll, we're pulling out tomorrow morning," I said, sipping on my juice and Gin.

Doll sipped on her drink through a straw. "You know that I tucked your cousin into bed like he was my big baby. I did a little straightening up before I took off to come down to the club tonight too." She slurped up all the liquor in her glass in one big pull.

Doll looked so foxy the way she sucked on the straw, to the point that it made me want to fuck her so bad.

"I can see your hickey clear now," I'd mentioned, mad that I wasn't the one who gave it to her. Eager to change the subject, she ignored me prying.

"What are you two doing with so much cash money up there in the room like that?" Quickly I looked into her eyes. Unnecessarily curious of our expenditures, she questioned, "Are you guys into drug dealing?" Doll remotely stared wearily at me, concerned. Her eyes seemed to have changed colors in the light.

Even if she was concerned it still wasn't none of her business, about what went on with us or what's in the green backpack, the least she knew the better off she was.

"We're out here to do some investing and a little gambling," I stated meekly to throw her off. "Doll, you didn't touch nothing did you?" I had to ask, unsmiling. Now I was the one doing the questioning.

"Vonny look!" She looked embarrassingly ill at ease with herself, with me, and this whole conversation.

"I'm just saying?" I said, giving her a strong gesture from my eyes.

Doll stood up ready to give me a piece of her mind. "Vonny!" she screamed as if she'd been scorned, as if her feelings were hurt.

From the way her pen and pad hit the table she was mad at me. I knew that I struck a nerve, but didn't care because I had over $200,000 dollars in cash up in the room. This wasn't the place nor time to start getting into the subtraction business. Not right now anyways.

"I am not a thief!" she tried to yell and get angry but I wasn't buying it. She was faking. "Just because I date here and there and work inside this club doesn't mean that I'm a scandalous ass bitch, Vonny. And yes I do know how to dance, and yes I do take off my clothes up there sometimes. I'm grown!" she scolded. Doll was on a roll now and I loved it. She got sexier by the minute. I put an ice cube in my mouth and listened to her like I really cared what she was talking about. At the end of the day Doll is a whore; because prostitutes lived for the moment, a whore is never to be trusted. Not now, not ever.

"Excuse me, let me go use the restroom," I stated, casually standing up to go relieve myself.

When I returned, Doll was ready to talk some more.

"I'm serious Vonny and you may not believe what I'm about to tell you, but it's the truth! I don't gotta lie." Doll held both of my hands in between hers so that we could talk, really talk. "I own my own home and have owned it ever since I graduated from college. I drive a Lexus. And get a brand new one every year, actually. So Vonny, I don't need to steal from you. You and Lefty are nothing but dope dealers to me that are promised a cell in the penitentiary some day. You're going to fall off like all the rest of the one's I've known. If you asked me, Vonny? Since I have a lot of major connections in this city, maybe you'll let me help you one way or another and put some of that money to good use." She still held my hands cupped inside of hers. After mine started to sweat I quickly pulled away. "What's the matter?" she asked.

"My hands be getting sweaty sometimes, whenever I get excited about something. I got sweaty palms, Doll," I explained. "That's an embarrassment I've dealt with ever since I was a kid."

Being that Doll was on a roll, there was no stopping her now from talking.

"So what, your hands sweat Vonny, you're cute and a very handsome guy. You also have a beautiful personality from what I've seen," she said softly, as she grabbed a hold of my hands again, and smiled. "So why don't you let me help you apply that money into something productive, something useful, something real?"

"Doll look! It's obvious that you don't even know me. And I do strongly apologize for accusing you of being scandalous..."

She started to cry at my hardness. Reaching across the table I handed her my bandana to wipe her face with.

"Don't cry on me, Doll. I didn't mean to hurt your feelings." *Women are just too damn sensitive,* I thought.

"Thank you," she said, after she had blown her nose on my rag. "I'm just sick and tired of being down rated. This scent is the reason why I'd walked into your room, Vonny. I just love the way this cologne smells." Doll carefully dried out one eye so the mascara wouldn't drip. "You see that guy over there," she gestured, raising her arm to point.

"Who?" I asked, quickly looking around hoping that she wasn't insinuating the transvestite behind the bar staring in our direction, particularly at me.

"No that one!" she pointed to a guy as big as a professional football player. He was light skinned, mixed with black, with curly wavy hair and he definitely worked out because his arms looked about twenty inches on soft. "He's my second cousin," she mentioned. Doll pointed out everybody in the bar who was either

her cousin or someone she was related too. I glanced around the joint.

"It seems to me that this is more like a family business than anything else."

Instantly, she raised her hand for one of her cousins to come over to our table. "Angela, this is a good friend of mine named Vonny. Vonny this is Angie, my first cousin." Doll introduced us in a respectful manner. She had a good vibe that I was good people. But she didn't have a clue who I truly was and what I'd just done a few hours ago. Like her, I too understood the value of secrecy.

"Vonny my great grandfather went by the name of Joe Adonis. He was a ladies' man back in his day. I never got to meet him, though. I was born right after the federale's killed him." She seemed so at home in this seedy domestic surrounding that I even began to sustain myself with its warming comfort. A short time later Angie brought over a big basket of fried chicken wings with Ranch dressing and more drinks to wash it down with. We talked for hours and hours until the early morning sky burned through, then after our stomachs were stuffed we both felt gravid and tipsy. Doll and I said our good-byes and agreed to meet back up again someday. She was dope and a lot of fun. It was seven that morning when we finally decided to part our separate ways.

Even though we had fun laughing and talking all night long, for some strange reason I didn't trust Doll. We were from two totally different worlds. Being from one of the most powerful crime families in the world she was an Italian half breed, with still that corrupted bad blood that Capo Dona warned me to stay away from.

I on the other hand was just a measly apprentice just starting out for an elite underground organization. Being that Doll went to bed with my homeboy, never would we ever be intimate sexually, or any other shape, form, or fashion. Our connection would always be like classic irony. We would always just be friends. After that night I preferred it like that. Good friends were hard to find nowadays.

LAST CHAPTER

When I returned to the suite, Lefty was already up ordering breakfast from room service. I glanced at the television, noticing a movie was on pause.

"You want something?" he asked.

"I'm too tired to eat right now," I wearily uttered, making my way towards my sleeping quarters. *I haven't been to sleep all night*, I thought to myself, falling head first on a soft king size bed. I quickly fogged out with the cell phone gun clutched tightly in my fist.

I'd woke with a slight hangover. My throat felt like a giant mothball was stuck it deep up in my esophagus. The clock on the wall read 2:05 P.M. After a short glance, I noticed that somebody placed my luggage neatly at the foot of my bed. At first I panicked, then felt relaxed once I spotted the green backpack. To ease my mind, I leaned forward and peeped inside to be sure that the money was still there. It was good.

I'd slept longer than I intended too, so I jumped up, and headed to the bathroom to freshen up. I shaved, took a shit, and then jumped in a steamy hot bath. Once finished, while brushing my teeth, Lefty came into the bathroom.

"Vonny guess what!"

"What?"

"I'm in love, fool."

"With who?" I questioned, brushing my tongue.

"With Doll! Who else?" He seemed happy. "Vonny, good looking out on that one."

As I was washing and rinsing out my mouth, I heard a voice.

"Vonny... Oh, so we meet again?" Doll surprised the hell out of me. She was smiling from ear to ear.

Her and Lefty were both looking extremely comfortable in their soft 100% white cotton robes, which were complements of the hotel. In the living room the stereo was playing a soulful Jazz song by the group Incognito. The sultry sounds was playing at a nice relaxing volume, sounding as if the band was actually performing live.

"Did anybody pay the bill?" I bluntly asked, since it was well past check out hours.

Doll held Lefty around his waist.

"I put my foot on it before I came up," she said quickly, kissing Lefty on the back of his neck.

Why would she spend $1,000 on us like that? This girl got me confused, I thought, *something's definitely going on that I don't know about. In this day and age people just don't go out of their way to do something for nothing.*

"Doll, what's the catch? What is it that you want?" I injected. She knew what I was getting at. Doll's a whore, so Lefty knew not to interfere and not to take sides against me over her. He also didn't know that last night Doll and I had a long grownup conversation, so we were both quite fond of one another.

"Vonny, chill," she exclaimed. "Carla downstairs and the hotel lobby clerk are good friends of mine. We went to high school together. Unfortunately, in this city it ain't what you know, it's who you know," she grumbled defensively, stomping out of the room very mad.

It was silent for a few seconds. I turned to Lefty.

"Man, you need to end whatever it is that you got going on with that girl. What happens in Vegas, needs to stay in Vegas!"

"What'cha mean?" he asked concerned, as he rolled a morning blunt for us to smoke on.

I don't think that he knew Doll was a blue blooded girl with an independent hustle. She made her money aggressively and was connected to this city in more ways than one.

"Homey, just get rid of the girl! Okay? Please! She's bad news, Man," I said, slipping on a white Polo T-shirt. "This girl could lead us into some major problems, maybe not right now, but in the long run things can get a little out of hand."

"Homey, you're trippin'!" he shot back, licking the end of a tobacco leaf. "Here man take this. Me and Doll is going out. I like her, Vonny."

Lefty put the blunt on the counter then took off. I'll just have to get over it. When I thought about things, I was the one who hooked them two up, so if they liked each other, then let them be. Lefty was a good friend to have because he wasn't the nosey type.

He knew that I was coming out here to Las Vegas for something and not once did he ever question my gangster. He just simply packed his bags and took off with me. I respected him for that. He also never asked whose car I was driving either. All he knew was that I drove a Acura Legend and rode a Ducati motorcycle, he also never once, which I found amazing ask me about the money in the green backpack with over $200,000 in it. Without him even knowing about it, Lefty was deeply involved in a murder conspiracy that involved two L.A. crime petty fiefdoms, where an unknown gunman had emptied his clip into both victims close range, and he's still on the run, which has left the authorities with no clues for a criminal prosecution.

They have no traces of evidence, so I counted my blessings because good friends are hard to find nowadays. Secrecy is power. Lefty Bull's loyalty will make me do things for him that I wouldn't normally do for another person. Well, except the familial.

Since Doll and Lefty were both gone. I was home alone and hadn't eaten anything, called room service, then opened the door to the terrace to allow some fresh air to get in. A song by Jay-Z was beating softly through the stereo speakers, so I sat outside a few minutes, listening to the melody and his lyrics. It was my intentions to relax before my brunch arrived.

"Room service!" she greeted, letting herself into the suite with her own key. My brunch was on a little food cart that Carla was pushing.

"Carla?" I said, surprised. "Thank you! You on housekeeping and catering too?" I teased. "Please set the tray over there." I politely insisted, noticing she was in the same white outfit she'd had on the day before.

She looked to be a hard worker, and had a passion for the job. She said she put in long hours on her detail to be sure that things ran productive and according to plan. Her hair was pulled back tight in a bun, which brought out her pretty feminine features. She was a curvaceous little thang, who looked like she exercised a lot.

"If you don't mine, Doll paid for the suite an extra night." Sweat began to moisten her forehead a little. "It's hot up here!" she fussed, using the back of her hand to wipe sweat from her face. "Boy this is Vegas, it gets hot out here." Carla walked over to the air conditioner to turn it on.

"You work too hard!" I said, as she poured my coffee.

"If I didn't, then who else is gonna make you feel at home while at the Plaza." She sighed, smiling. "My parents are old. They don't move around like they used to back in the old days, Mr. Plot!"

"No it's Vonny," I laughed.

"Okay Vonny. There's a telegram that came in earlier today from a Ms. Miranda." Carla handed me the letter. "Also, the daily paper comes with our brunch," she explained before easing out of the door.

No later than the door was shut did I devour two of the glazed donuts on the brunch cart. I'd been ripping and running around so much that I had no time to relax. For a different spin on my day, I opened the newspaper to the Business & Finance page. I wanted to check up on my ETFs stock while sipping on the house's coffee. Because Miranda had never written me before, for some strange reason the butterflies in my stomach made my nerves bad. *I'm out on location, working. That girl shouldn't have any knowledge, information, nor idea about where I'm at, which only meant one thing----that something was definitely wrong back in California.* I quickly torn open the seal on the envelope and smelled sweet perfume on the only page enclosed. The letter read:

Dear Vonny,

Unfortunately, you must return to the mansion immediately! Always remember that my father is forever extremely proud of you. After you receive this note "Do Not" call. Also, do not engage yourself in any business transactions what-so-ever, of any kind. Use your own ingenuity to understand this urgent message. I need you here with me, right now. I'm very scared and don't even know what to do.

Miranda

After shockingly reading the letter from Miranda over and over, I was devastated. I couldn't think straight. To help the nerves, I lit up the chronic Lefty gave me earlier. As I read the letter one more time, the part about her being very scared made my heart skip a beat. My mental and emotional feelings were strained with tension so thick that I could've cut through it with a knife.

Right away I scribbled something down to leave Lefty a note of my whereabouts, plus I didn't want him to worry about me. On my way out, I swung my Gucci bag over one shoulder and the green backpack over the other, counted out ten $100 big faces for the homey to have just in case his cash got low.

While waiting for the elevator, I was going through something from Miranda's letter. To avoid not bumping into Carla, I snuck around to the back exit, and then crept to the front of the building to wait for the bellhop to bring me my car. When he arrived with the Audi fully intact, I slid him a healthy tip, quickly slammed my belongings inside the trunk, jumped in the driver seat, and put the pedal to the metal.

I stopped for gas to fill up, then drove back to California at about 70 MPH. I thought about the love connection I'd made back there between Doll and Lefty, praying by now he knew that he was now rolling with a thug. For some odd reason they seemed made for each other. *Just be careful homey*, I thought to myself, because Doll was a very experienced girl.

After setting the cruise control, I put Biggie Small's CD in and started singing along.

"I'm going... going... back... back ...to... Cali ...Cali!" At four o'clock, the car's thermometer read 95° from the hot sun, but I knew I'd be back in Orange County around eight that evening. With that thought in mind, I crossed over the desert, feeling free as a bird with no regret of the sin I'd committed the day before.

A picture of the snitch, Mobie "Dique" Lewis stuck in my head. What clicked the most was the way he tried sucking up his last breath of life. I'm pretty satisfied with myself because no one will ever suspect who it was that assassinated Mobie and his lieutenant. My complexion is a tanned-bronze color. If worst came to worst, witnesses would swear up and down that a white guy had committed the killing. A white man killing two black gang members held no weight in a today's society. A white man can get away with murder, where as a black man would get a life sentence in prison for a crumb of cocaine. Where else would they do that besides in America.

From a glimpse, the endless hot desert sand was sprouting its cactus plants all over the place. Plants were accustomed to the blistering heat, but I wasn't. Though I had no idea at the time of what I was getting myself into back at the Castle; I do know one thing for sure, things were getting more and more serious every day.

These people were my roots. Who are they for real? I thought, putting this whole fuckin' city in my rear view to go find out.

PART II ... Coming Soon

About the Author:

Compton Blue wrote this book from prison. It is a passionate work of fiction. Names, characters, incidents and places that's portrayed in this novel are products of the author's imagination or are used fictitiously.

We Help You Self-Publish Your Book

We Help You Self-Publish Your Book
Crystell Publications has worked hard to build our quality brand. Regardless of your status, our team will help you get to print. Our BLOW OUT prices are for serious authors only. And surely with fees like these, every author who desires to be published can. **Don't have all your money? .... No Problem!** *Ask About our Payment Plans*

Crystal Perkins-Stell, MHR
Essence Magazine Bestseller
We Give You Books!
PO BOX 8044 / Edmond – OK 73083
www.crystalstell.com
(405) 414-3991

Our competitor's Cheapest Plans- **AuthorHouse** Legacy Plan $1299.00- 8 books **Xilibris** Professional Plan $1249.00 10 bks, **iUniverse** Premier Plan $1299.00-5 bks
Hey! Stop Wishing, and get your book to print NOW!!!

–Recession Big Flex Options 100 Books–					
Option A	**Option B**	**Option C**	**Option D**	**E-Book**	**Option F**
$1399.00	$1299.00	$1199.00	$839.00	$695.00	$775.00
255-275	205-250	200 -80	75 - 60	255 pages	50 or less
Grind Plans 25 & E-Book		**Hustle Hard**	**Respect The Code**		**313 Deal**
Order Extra Books		$899.00	$869.00		$839.00
		255-275pg	250 -205		200 -80
Insanity Plans 5-10 Books & E-Book		**Psycho**	**Spastic**		**Mental**
Extra Books Can Be Ordered		$679.00	$659.00		$649.00
		225-250pg	200-220		199- 100
All Manuscript Options except the E-Books include:					
2 Proofs Publisher/Printer Copy, Mink Magazine Advertisement, Book Cover, ISBN #, Conversion, Typeset, Correspondence, Masters, 8 hrs Consultation					

$100.00 E-book upload only
$275.00-Book covers/Authors input
$269.00-Book covers/ templates
$190.00 and up Websites
$375.00, book trailers on Youtube

$75 Can't afford edits, Spell-check
$499 Flat Rate Edits Exceeds 210 add 1.50 pp
$200-Typeset Book Format PDF File
$200 and up / Type Manuscript Call for details

We're Killing The Game.

These titles are done by self-published authors. **They are not published by, nor signed to Crystell Publications.** You control the money and they experience. No more paying Vanity Presses $8 to $10 per book! We Give You Books at Cost. **Editing Is Offered For An Extra Fee- If Waved, We Print What You Submit!**

Printed in Great Britain
by Amazon

39557978R00076